D0678197

The Mystery at Blue Moon Stables

Sidney Sinclair Adventure #1

Kathryn B. Butler

Copyright © 2013 Katherine Bailey

Published by What About Jelly Publishing

Cover art by Josh Petty

All rights reserved. This book or any portion thereof may not be reproduced or used in any manner whatsoever without the express written permission of the author. This is a work of fiction. Any resemblance to persons, living or dead, is purely coincidental.

ISBN: 0615901557

ISBN-13: 978-0615901558

DEDICATION

I dedicate this book to all those who love the smell of a barn
and the feel of a horse underneath them. And most of all, to
Little Bit, who taught me how to ride.

CONTENTS

ACKNOWLEDGMENTS

This book would never have made it into print without the help of my family, my readers, my horses, my fellow authors, and my sister. Thank you to everyone who made this possible.

CHAPTER 1

A Reunion

"Good morning, world!" Sidney Sinclair yelled, bursting through the front door. She ran down the porch steps and into the sun with an enthusiastic energy only the first day of summer can provide.

She skipped across the yard, her feet skimming over the short grass, and skidded to a stop just long enough to glance longingly over her neighbor's fence. The plastic cover was still stretched over the pool. The May air felt warm against her skin, but not hot enough for swimming yet. She sighed sadly, but her frown turned to a smile when she saw the Abbots' two dogs, Snapper and Sam, grinning up at her from inside the fence. Sam jumped up and hung his paws over the gate, his tongue lolling comically from the side of his mouth.

Sidney was tempted, but she didn't go in to say hello to her canine friends. Instead, she crossed the carefully mown grass on the front lawn and climbed the steps of her neighbor's front porch. She wanted to say hello to a human friend she had been missing for quite some time.

Sidney paused at the Abbots' front door to check her reflection in one of the four glass panes on its upper half. She had pulled her ginger-colored hair back with a white ribbon that morning and put on her best jeans and a white polo shirt. She was attempting to look presentable for Mrs. Abbot, her best friend's mother. Mrs. Abbot wasn't Sidney's biggest fan.

After adjusting her ribbon, Sidney knocked politely. It took a moment for the door to open. When it did, a pretty middle-aged woman stood in front of her. Her makeup had already been applied for the day, and she smiled hesitantly at Sidney with red-painted lips.

"Hello, Sidney." Mrs. Abbot kept the door nearly closed, only peering through a small gap.

Sidney did her best to smile encouragingly back. Mrs. Abbot didn't exactly approve of Sidney's friendship with her daughter, Jane, but Sidney was determined to prove to Mrs. Abbot how much she had grown up since the previous summer. A lot of things had changed.

"Good morning, Mrs. Abbot. Is Jane at home?"

Mrs. Abbot hesitated for a moment, glancing over her shoulder, then sighed and opened the door a little wider, gesturing for Sidney to come in. "Yes, dear. I suppose you two will be getting into some... adventures today?"

Sidney frowned. "Oh, don't say it like that, Mrs. Abbot. No adventures like last summer. You know I promised to behave from now on and... act my age." The last part had been Mrs. Abbot's suggestion, but Sidney didn't remind her of the fact. "And Jane, too. Jane would *never* go back on a promise."

Mrs. Abbot raised an eyebrow as Sidney shuffled past

her and into the spotless entryway. Gleaming white tile floors led to a small kitchen at the back of the house and Sidney could hear the clinking of dishes and running water coming from that direction.

"Don't shuffle your feet, Sidney," Mrs. Abbot said. "Jane is cleaning up after breakfast. You'll have to wait until she's finished."

Sidney nodded as calmly as she could, but she felt a shiver of excitement race up her spine. Jane attended a boarding school a few hours away. The pair had gotten together over the short breaks for holidays, of course, but this would be their first extended visit since last summer.

"That's fine, Mrs. Abbot. I can just wait out on the porch if you want."

Mrs. Abbot looked at her appraisingly. Sidney knew she wouldn't want anyone to think she would be less than welcoming to a visitor. It wouldn't be proper, but…. Mrs. Abbot glanced back toward the kitchen then looked down at her freshly mopped floors.

"That would be fine. Jane might be a few minutes."

Sidney gladly stepped back outside, letting the front door bang shut behind her. She breathed the fresh air deeply to try and rid her nose of the chemical smell of bleach and lemon-scented cleaner, a smell which often filled the inside of the Abbots' home.

She plopped down in a reclining wooden chair beside the front door. The chair was part of an expensive outdoor furniture set the Abbots had purchased a few weeks earlier. Sidney never could understand why they spent so much time and money improving their yard. Jane was the only member of the family who spent time outdoors.

While she waited for Jane, she daydreamed about all the adventures they would have in the coming weeks. She and Jane always had the best adventures together. Exploring the old barn, training Snapper and Sam to do amazing tricks, and even better....

Jane banged through the door and let it slam shut loudly behind her, interrupting Sidney's thoughts. An incoherent, but obviously angry, shout came from somewhere in the house and Sidney grinned.

"I take it your mom isn't happy to see me?" she said to her friend after they exchanged quick hugs and looked each other up and down. Jane had grown a lot over the last few months. She was a just a tad taller than Sidney now, and her long blonde hair hung almost to the middle of her back.

Jane rolled her blue eyes dramatically. "No. Plus, she has a house rule about slamming doors. She says it shatters her nerves."

Sidney giggled. Just about everything seemed to shatter Mrs. Abbot's nerves.

"Come on," Sidney said, pulling her friend down the front steps and across the lawn toward the backyard. "We need to catch up, but I have to say hello to Snapper and Sam first."

"What do you mean, silly?" Jane said smiling. "Snapper and Sam are always here. You can say hello to them anytime."

"With your mother here?" Sidney's eyes widened. "I don't think so. If she found me in your backyard, she'd probably call the cops."

Jane giggled and squeezed Sidney's hand. "She would not."

Sidney unlatched the gate and Jane followed her into the backyard. The two German Shepherds met them with wet kisses from their long tongues and a few barks, which Jane tried to quiet desperately. "Shush, Snapper! Do you want to go back to behavioral school?"

The dogs whimpered and wiggled, begging for attention, but they quieted down. After they'd tired of kisses and petting, Sam slunk away to lay on the warm concrete by the pool, and Snapper brought her red rubber ball over and dropped it in front of Sidney. She rubbed the big dog's nose and tossed the ball across the yard for her to fetch.

The girls spent the next half hour or so catching up on events that had occurred since their last in-person visit during Christmas break. They had exchanged letters, emails, texts, and even a few phone calls while separated, but nothing could beat talking over all the juicy gossip in person.

Sidney mostly listened at first while Jane told her about all the boarding school drama. Jane seemed to love her school, Graceland Academy.

"I wish I loved school as much as you, Jane," Sidney said wistfully. She attended Walker Middle School and rarely enjoyed the experience.

Jane shrugged, her face turning a bit pink. "I don't always love it. It gets boring sometimes. And I do miss my family."

Sidney glanced at the Abbots' house. She could see Mrs. Abbot peering at them suspiciously through a back window.

Jane sighed and shook her head, the sun glinting off her pretty blonde hair. "Mom still doesn't trust you."

Sidney shrugged and ignored the comment. She had a feeling Mrs. Abbot would never trust her no matter what she did, so she changed the subject quickly.

"Did you get my letter about the stables?" Sidney felt like she would burst with excitement whenever she thought about the stables. She had been watching closely from her bedroom window for the last two months while their new neighbor across the road, Cindy Fitzpatrick, built stables and then a riding arena. Now that school was out, she was eager to go over and see the new riding stables up close.

"Mom says the stables will be opening up next week for classes. Mrs. Fitzpatrick's been accepting students for months now and everything is finally ready," Jane said. "It's going to be a busy place from what I hear."

"Guess what?"

"You know I don't like guessing. What is it?" Jane asked. She turned to look at Sidney seriously. Her pale blue eyes and snub nose gave her face a childish appearance, which she complained about often. People usually thought Sidney was older than Jane when it was actually just the opposite. Jane was already eleven and Sidney's eleventh birthday wouldn't be until August.

"I'm one of the students starting lessons next week," Sidney revealed proudly.

"You'll be taking lessons at Mrs. Fitzpatrick's stables?" Jane asked, her jaw dropping.

Sidney nodded. "Blue Moon Stables."

"Is that what she's named the stables? Why Blue Moon?" Jane asked.

"Mom asked her when we went to sign up for lessons. She said that you only get the chance to live out your dream once in a blue moon. Owning stables and teaching kids to ride is her dream."

"Wow, Sid," Jane replied, looking awed. "So you're going to be taking riding lessons. That's so exciting." She smiled at Sidney, but it didn't quite reach her eyes.

"Mrs. Fitzpatrick was so nice," Sidney replied. "She seems like she'll be a great teacher. I can't wait to go and meet the horses and see which one I'll be riding. I wonder if I'll ride the same one every week or if it'll be a different horse each time?"

Jane shrugged and looked at the ground.

"Is this going to be another one of your throwaway hobbies, Sid?"

Sidney looked offended and put her hands on her hips. "I don't know what you mean, Jane."

"You know exactly what I mean. You have a new one every summer. The first summer we met you started taking dancing lessons with me and it was all you talked about. You were tired of it by the end of the summer. Have you ever danced again?"

Sidney frowned. "You know I haven't. Dancing is your thing." Jane was a beautiful dancer. She took ballet and jazz classes and spent hours practicing. She performed in recitals often during the school year. In fact, the year before she had starred in the Christmas ballet at Graceland Academy.

"The next summer it was art," Jane continued. "You spent the entire summer sketching and painting. Have you picked up a paintbrush since that summer?"

Sidney paused to think about it, then she shook her head.

"Then it was swimming. You were going to be an Olympic swimmer, if I remember correctly."

Sidney laughed. "Okay. Enough. You might have a point. But this is different."

Jane rolled her eyes and pushed Sidney playfully. "Yeah, right."

Sidney started to laugh but stopped short when she felt a tickle on her bare leg.

"Eeew!" Jane squealed, pointing.

Sidney picked a beetle from her leg and threw it to the ground. Sam leapt up and pounced on the scurrying bug before Sidney could stop him, squashing it under his big paw. Jane shuddered, a look of disgust on her face.

"It's just a bug," Sidney said. "At least it wasn't a spider."

"That's true, but you know I hate bugs. All of them. And that was disgusting Sam." She shook a finger at the dog, but he didn't seem to notice.

Sidney sighed. She'd seen Jane almost go into hysterics over a wasp. It had landed on her arm for just a moment before buzzing away and she'd almost fainted. Another time she'd run screaming from the shed because a bumblebee had gotten tangled in her hair. She'd cried for hours afterward and refused to go outside again for days. Sometimes Jane was scarier around insects than the insects themselves, even the ones with stingers.

"Have you met Mrs. Fitzpatrick's son, Bryan?" Jane asked, shooing Sam away. The dog trotted off to take up his place by the pool again.

Sidney shook her head. "He wasn't there when we went to sign up for lessons. We didn't even get to go into the barn or the arena or anything. Mom said Mrs. Fitzpatrick was busy and we should get out of her hair. We only talked to her for a few minutes and Mom signed the paperwork."

"My mom told me he's about our age. She said we should invite him to play with us sometime. He's having trouble making friends here."

Sidney frowned and bit her lip. "Mrs. Fitzpatrick suggested the same thing."

"Well, I think we should. We could invite him to come swimming when it's warm enough."

Sidney wrinkled her nose. She didn't want some neighbor boy interrupting their time together. The summer months always seemed to fly by so fast, and she didn't like how Jane seemed more interested in Bryan than the horses.

"Maybe," she said, and took Jane's hand. "Let's go for a walk. Tell me about Rachel, that girl from your French class. The one you wrote me about. Are you getting along better with her now?"

* * *

When lunchtime approached, the two were forced to go their separate ways. Mrs. Abbot wanted to take Jane into town for a haircut, and Sidney's mother called her in for lunch. Mrs. Sinclair had made grilled cheese sandwiches and French fries.

"Your grilled cheese sandwiches are the best, Mom," Sidney said, a glob of gooey cheese dripping from her chin.

"Wipe your face, Sidney," her mother replied, taking a seat at the kitchen table across from her. Her mother worked as a teacher at the same school Sidney attended, Walker Middle, so she would be off for most of the summer, too.

Sidney admired her mother more than anyone else she knew. Right now, Mrs. Sinclair's ginger-colored hair, which Sidney had inherited, was swept up in a neat bun. The spattering of freckles across her nose and her sparkling sea green eyes made her appear young and carefree, and that's how she acted most of the time, too. Sidney sighed enviously as she stared across the table at her mother. She hoped she would grow up to look like her. She wished often, and in vain, that she had inherited her mother's beautiful green eyes, but she hadn't. Her own eyes were brown, and a dull, boring brown at that.

"I can't wait to start my riding lessons. I was telling Jane all about the stables this morning."

"Really? Well, you two will get to see them for yourselves next Wednesday."

"I don't think Jane is taking lessons, Mom. In fact, she seemed a little jealous when I told her that I was already signed up."

Sidney's mom raised her eyebrows.

"Actually, I have it on good authority that she is taking lessons. In fact, she's signed up for the very same class you are."

Sidney's eyes lit up. "Who told you that?"

"Mrs. Abbot. She called about an hour ago. She went over to have coffee with Mrs. Fitzpatrick this morning. The two have become good friends since Mrs. Fitzpatrick moved in. She found out that you and Jane are in the same class. A small class of ten to twelve year olds."

"Why did she call to tell you that?" Sidney asked, a bit worried. Mrs. Abbot didn't call her mother often. When she did, it was usually to complain about something she thought Sidney had done wrong.

Sidney's mother smiled at her. "Don't you know? She's still upset about your 'treasure hunt' last summer. She didn't enjoy filling all the holes you and Jane dug in her backyard and re-planting all her precious flowers. You know how she is about that yard."

Sidney frowned. "We thought we found a map. We were sure the treasure was there somewhere. Besides, I promised just this morning that I wouldn't get into any trouble or get Jane into any trouble. We won't dig up anything. Cross my heart."

She crossed her heart with her finger and stared solemnly at her mother.

Her mother stifled a laugh and almost choked on the last bite of her grilled cheese sandwich. "I know that, but Mrs. Abbot isn't so sure."

Her mother got up from the table, her plate empty, and collected Sidney's empty plate as well. She took them to the sink and started loading the dishwasher.

"Have you done your chores today, Sid?" she asked as Sidney sidled toward the back door.

Sidney shook her head guiltily.

"Herbert doesn't like waiting for his breakfast until lunchtime," her mother said, her hands on her hips. "Neither would you, right?"

Sidney shook her head. It was a good point. "Sorry, Mom."

Her mother nodded and pointed toward the laundry room where Herbert's food and water bowl were kept. Sidney found Herbert sitting in front of his bowl, staring at it angrily.

After pouring some dry cat food into his bowl, Sidney looked at him hesitantly for a moment before reaching down to stroke his back. He looked so soft and fluffy she couldn't resist, but she knew he hated it. He was the only cat she knew who hated to be petted. Normally, he would lay back his orange ears and hiss or run away. Only when he was distracted by food would he allow her to touch his silky fur.

After she got her fill of petting him, she took his water bowl to the kitchen and filled it at the sink. Herbert had finished eating and was gone by the time she got back to the laundry room. Before her mom could ask her to do another chore, Sidney slipped quietly out the back door.

She stayed in the backyard, swinging idly on the tire swing her father had rigged up for her, while she waited for the Abbots to return. Mrs. Abbot's blue sedan finally pulled into their driveway about an hour later. It had hardly stopped before Jane was out and running. She was headed toward the front of Sidney's house, probably to knock on the front door, but Sidney intercepted her halfway through the yard.

Jane's blue eyes gleamed with excitement. "You'll never guess what I just found out!"

Sidney wanted to yell it out as loudly as she could, but she just managed to hold her tongue. Jane looked so excited to tell her the news she couldn't bear to ruin the surprise by telling her she already knew. "What is it, Jane?" she asked, trying to sound curious.

"Mom's just told me that I'm going to be taking riding lessons, too! And guess what? It gets even better!"

Sidney grasped Jane's hands and bounced up and down on her toes. "How can it get better than that?"

"We're going to be in the same class!" Jane yelled.

Both girls squealed with excitement.

* * *

The next few days passed quickly. Jane and Sidney spent most of their time together, much to Mrs. Abbot's disapproval, and most of it was spent talking about horses and wondering what their first riding lesson would be like.

When Wednesday morning finally came, Sidney jumped out of bed and thundered down the stairs. Her mother was brewing coffee at the kitchen counter.

"Somebody's up early," her mother said. "And I think I know the reason."

Sidney grinned and went over to the refrigerator to get the carton of milk. She poured out a tall glass and sat down at the table.

"You know your riding lesson isn't until eleven, Sid?"

Sidney nodded. "I know. I just couldn't sleep for another second."

Mrs. Sinclair ruffled Sidney's already messy shoulder-length hair and leaned down to give her a kiss on the cheek. "I guess you'll need a hearty breakfast. You need to keep up your strength when you're riding horses, right?"

Sidney nodded and got up to peer out the window. She let out a sigh of relief. She had discussed the possibility of rain with Jane. They were afraid it would ruin their lesson if it rained, but there wasn't a cloud in the sky. The sun was already peeking its head over the tree line in the backyard, and it looked like it was going to be a perfect day.

"When's Dad coming home again?" Sidney asked. A sudden pang of sadness shot through her. She would have to call and tell him she was taking riding lessons. He probably didn't even know. He hadn't been home for a visit in over a month.

Although he had explained it numerous times, Sidney could never really understand what he did for a living. She knew he worked on machinery and on a contract basis. He had to travel a lot because he had to go wherever the company he had a contract with was located. This time, his company was working in Philadelphia. They would be there for the rest of the summer, and this was the farthest away he'd been in a long time. He usually came home at least on the weekends, but this job was too important for him to leave.

Her mother paused. "Soon, Sid. In fact, very soon."

Sidney smiled. "Can we cook him a special breakfast when he gets here? Waffles with whipped cream and strawberries?"

"Of course, Sid. And we'll make a special dinner, too. Like we always do."

"Have you ever taken riding lessons, Mom?"

She shook her head and filled a coffee cup to the brim

with steaming coffee. "Not exactly. I rode my cousin's horse on occasion, but I never had a formal lesson. I always wanted to, though."

"You should take lessons now," Sidney said, pulling herself up to sit on the counter. She liked to sit on the kitchen counter in the mornings and watch her mother make breakfast.

Her mother laughed and pushed a strand of hair behind her ear.

"I don't think so, Sid." She handed Sidney a mixing bowl and a spoon and gestured toward the cabinet. "Time for you to make pancakes."

CHAPTER 2

The First Riding Lesson

Sidney trembled with excitement as Mrs. Fitzpatrick led them into the barn. Sidney and Jane held hands nervously and looked around with wide eyes. They were walking so closely behind their instructor, they almost bumped into her when she stopped suddenly in the middle of the barn aisle.

"Careful," Mrs. Fitzpatrick said with a smile.

The barn smelled of hay, wood shavings, and horses. Sidney inhaled deeply. It smelled like heaven to her.

"We have three stalls on the left," Mrs. Fitzpatrick said, gesturing to three occupied stalls on her left, "and three on the right. As you can see, only four of our stalls are occupied at the moment."

Four horses looked out curiously over the half doors of the stalls, their ears pricked forward with interest. They watched the newcomers as curiously as the girls watched them.

Mrs. Fitzpatrick pointed to the first stall on the left. "Sidney, you'll be riding Jasper."

Sidney went over and stood just out of his reach, hesitant at his large size. He was taller and leaner than the other horses in the barn. "He's beautiful."

His black coat gleamed with health, and the large

white stripe running down the center of his face reminded her of a lightning bolt. He nuzzled her hand in a friendly manner when she finally got up the courage to inch close enough to pat his soft nose.

"Don't worry," Mrs. Fitzpatrick said, noticing Sidney's nervousness. "You couldn't ask for a better horse. I bought him from another riding stable. He's been teaching children to ride for years."

Jane looked a bit afraid, too. She joined Sidney beside Jasper and approached him slowly, laying a hand on his warm neck. Her blue eyes had gotten very round. Mrs. Fitzpatrick pointed her to the mare in the next stall, an old flea-bitten gray with tired eyes.

"This is Misty," Mrs. Fitzpatrick said, going over to rub her neck. Misty hung her head over the stall door and closed her eyes. Her ears flopped comically down on either side of her head, almost like a dog's ears, when Mrs. Fitzpatrick scratched between them.

"She reminds me of Eeyore," Sidney whispered to Jane.

Jane giggled and elbowed Sidney. "Don't insult her."

Sidney decided within the first five minutes that she was going to like Mrs. Fitzpatrick. The riding instructor was an outdoorsy type with a long brown ponytail and hazel eyes. She appeared to be about the same age as Sidney's mother. She let the girls pet and talk to their horses for a few minutes before she led them off to the tack room to retrieve their grooming supplies and riding gear.

"After every lesson, you'll need to return your riding gear to the tack room," she said. "Sometimes, your riding gear will need to be cleaned. I'll teach you how to do that."

The girls nodded. Sidney sniffed and then inhaled

deeply. She couldn't decide if the stables smelled better or the tack room. The tack room had a wonderful leathery scent.

Mrs. Fitzpatrick gave them a short tour, showing them where everything was kept. The room was neat and orderly. Everything seemed to have a place. Sidney admired the gleaming saddles, which were set all in a row on saddle racks on the back wall. Bridles, halters, and lead ropes hung on pegs to their right, and in the left corner, grooming boxes set on the floor filled with grooming supplies.

"I never knew a barn could be so clean," Sidney said.

Mrs. Fitzpatrick only smiled in response, but Sidney could tell she was very pleased. She instructed the girls to choose a halter and lead rope for their horses. Sidney chose a pretty blue halter she thought would look good against Jasper's black coat and a soft, white lead rope. Jane chose a red halter and matching lead rope.

The two girls grabbed grooming buckets and headed back to the stalls. Their mothers stood in the barn aisle, waiting. They looked like they weren't sure whether to stay or go. Mrs. Sinclair appeared interested and was watching Mrs. Fitzpatrick carefully as she instructed the girls, but Mrs. Abbot looked uncomfortable and out of place.

Using Jasper, Mrs. Fitzpatrick showed the girls how to slip the halter over the horse's head and buckle it. Then, she snapped the lead rope onto the halter and opened the stall door, leading Jasper out into the aisle. He looked even bigger than he had in his stall, and Mrs. Abbot backed out of the barn, looking alarmed.

Mrs. Fitzpatrick hid a smile with her hand. "You can pull up a chair outside the arena if you want to stay and watch," she said to the girls' mothers, "or you can go home if you want. The girls are in good hands."

Mrs. Abbot smiled uncertainly and shifted her purse to her left shoulder. "Well, I suppose I'll go on home. I do have a few things I need to do. Is that all right, Jane?"

Jane barely glanced at her mother. "Of course, Mom."

Jane was used to her mother dropping her off for activities. As an avid dancer, Jane usually spent more time at the dance studio during the summer than at home.

"Sidney, what about you? Do you want me to stay?" Mrs. Sinclair asked.

Sidney shook her head. "No, that's okay, Mom. Jane and I can walk home together after the lesson."

Her mother nodded and came over to give her a quick hug. "Okay. Be careful, though, Sid."

Mrs. Abbot and Mrs. Sinclair left together. Sidney felt a little relieved and she could tell Jane did, too. They already felt nervous enough without having their mothers watch them ride!

Mrs. Fitzpatrick showed the girls how to cross tie Jasper in the barn aisle. A rope with a snap on the end hung from the wall on either side of the aisle.

"It's very easy. All you have to do is snap the ropes on either side to the horse's halter," Mrs. Fitzpatrick said.

She showed them how the ropes were attached to brass circles on the walls with bailing twine instead of being directly tied to them.

"That's in case a horse panics," she said. "If he panicked and pulled back on the ropes too hard, he could hurt himself. This way, if he panics and pulls back to the point of hurting himself, the twine will break and he'll be loose."

"Isn't that a bad thing?" Jane asked, her face pale.

"Not necessarily," Mrs. Fitzpatrick responded. "Most of the time, once they are loose, they calm down and are easily caught."

"Will Jasper break loose?" Sidney asked. He looked slightly bored. He stood with one back hoof propped up, and his bottom lip drooped a bit.

"I think he's asleep." Jane giggled.

Mrs. Fitzpatrick laughed, too. "He's resting. See how he has all his weight on three of his legs, and the other leg isn't holding any weight? He'll switch in a minute and let the opposite leg rest."

The girls watched, and in a moment, he switched his weight to the other side and propped up his other back hoof.

"To answer your question," Mrs. Fitzpatrick continued, "Jasper is very quiet. He's a steady horse. He's never tried to break loose, but it's always best to be safe around horses and take all the precautions you can. Some horses may get scared while they're cross-tied. Better safe than sorry, right?"

Sidney nodded and Mrs. Fitzpatrick handed her a brush from the grooming box. She showed them how to groom the horses starting with the currycomb. With the currycomb and all the brushes that followed, Mrs. Fitzpatrick started at the top of Jasper's neck and worked her way back toward his rump.

"He looked like he was already clean," Sidney commented, watching Mrs. Fitzpatrick closely.

"Even if your horse looks clean, you should always go over him again before you ride him. You don't want any dirt or burrs getting under the saddle. That could hurt the horse or irritate his skin and cause sores and such."

She pulled a metal pick out of the grooming box. Jane, who had been copying Mrs. Fitzpatrick's actions while grooming Misty, gasped. "What is that for? It looks dangerous."

Mrs. Fitzpatrick laughed again. Her laugh was light, bubbly and infectious. Sidney grinned. She liked it.

"No, Jane, not if used correctly," Mrs. Fitzpatrick responded. "It's a hoof pick. We use it to clean out a horse's hooves."

She leaned over and picked up Jasper's big hoof. The girls watched carefully while she showed them how to use it. Jasper had bits of mud and a piece of small gravel stuck in his hoof, but she scooped them out easily with the hoof pick.

"It is very important to keep your horse's hooves clean and free of rocks," Mrs. Fitzpatrick said, looking at them seriously to be sure they understood. "Rocks in their hooves can injure them and make them go lame."

They nodded solemnly. "There are so many rules," Jane sighed. "How will we ever remember them all?"

Mrs. Fitzpatrick smiled kindly. "Before long, it will all become second nature. But you never stop learning with horses. I've been riding for fifteen years and – "

"Can I ride Magic?" A loud voice interrupted.

Mrs. Fitzpatrick set Jasper's hoof down carefully and turned around to face the speaker with a frown. Jane and Sidney turned around, too.

A boy about their age stood a few feet away. He had close-cut brown hair and brown eyes with heavy brows above them. He would have been what Jane called "cute" if he hadn't had such a sour expression on his face. He frowned angrily and hunched his shoulders forward. He was quite a bit taller than Sidney and looked very muscular to be so young. The girls glanced at each other. Sidney raised her eyebrows. *This must be Bryan.*

"Sidney. Jane," Mrs. Fitzpatrick said, "this is my son, Bryan. I don't think you have met."

He nodded toward the two girls. His frown lifted a bit

when Jane gave a small wave in his direction, and Sidney thought she even glimpsed a ghost of a smile appear on his face, but it disappeared as soon as his mother spoke again.

"Yes, you can ride Magic today, Bryan. Be careful. He's a little jumpy."

Bryan rolled his eyes and stomped past them toward Magic's stall.

"Don't pay attention to him, girls. He isn't happy about moving here. He misses his friends back home and I'm afraid he's taking it out on everybody."

She brought saddles and bridles from the tack room and showed the girls how to tack up quickly. Then she led their horses into the riding arena, which was attached to the back of the barn, and tied them to the railing. She showed them the knot she used, a quick release knot, and taught them how to tie it.

"There's even a special way to tie a horse up," Sidney sighed dramatically. "I'll never remember all this."

The crunch of gravel beneath car tires and the blast of a car horn heralded the arrival of another riding student.

"That must be Jimmy," Mrs. Fitzpatrick said. "He's bringing his own horse. Why don't you two girls watch Bryan tack up while I go and help him unload Charlie from the trailer? You're riding English today, but Bryan will be riding Western, and tacking up Western is a little different."

"Will Jasper and Misty be okay out here by themselves?" Sidney asked, rubbing Jasper's neck. She was getting used to being so near to the big horse.

"I'll get Bryan to bring Magic out here. That way you can stay close to them," Mrs. Fitzpatrick said, patting Sidney on the shoulder. She headed off toward the barn looking a bit flustered.

"I wonder if we're her first lesson?" Jane whispered.

Sidney shrugged.

A few minutes later, Bryan came out into the arena leading Magic. He tied the horse, a big chestnut with four white socks, nearby and went back to retrieve his saddle pad, saddle, and bridle. He set the big square saddle pad carefully on the horse's back and showed the girls how to put the Western saddle on top and tie the cinch.

"It's called a girth in English and a cinch in Western riding," Bryan said. He seemed friendlier when he got to show off his riding knowledge, and Sidney noticed he seemed especially friendly toward Jane.

Sidney rolled her eyes at her friend, but Jane seemed to be eating it up. She was leaning forward and listening eagerly. Much more eagerly than she had listened to Mrs. Fitzpatrick.

As soon as Bryan finished tacking up, he led Magic to the middle of the arena and climbed up onto his back. Unlike Misty and Jasper, who looked bored and tired, Magic looked excited. His handsome ears were pricked forward, and he didn't seem able to stand still. His hooves moved constantly, stirring up a dusty cloud.

Jane glanced at Sidney with wide eyes. "I don't like this."

"I don't think he's supposed to be riding yet," Sidney replied, rubbing her eyes. They felt gritty with dirt. The cloud grew larger as the horse skittered around the arena, kicking up dust all the way. Bryan laughed and pulled the reins first to the right and then to the left, making Magic even more frantic.

The sound of hooves plodding sedately down the concrete barn aisle behind them distracted the girls. The arena gate creaked open and a blond boy leading a large bay gelding came in.

He wore an oversized cowboy hat and matching cowboy boots. He grinned at Bryan crookedly as Bryan steered the wild horse toward him. The girls jumped out of the way, hugging the arena rails as Magic careened past, but the blond boy didn't seem worried.

Magic stopped, snorting and blowing, just in front of the big bay's face. The newly arrived horse looked alarmed and backed up quickly. Bryan and other boy laughed.

"Bryan is such a showoff," Sidney whispered to Jane behind her hand.

But Jane wasn't paying attention to Jimmy. She was studying the new boy. "That must be Jimmy." She giggled. "He looks like he walked out of the old West."

Sidney nodded. After a few minutes of talking to Bryan, Jimmy looked in their direction. He tipped his cowboy hat and smiled crookedly again. Jane smiled back and waved.

She started to say something to Jimmy, but the exchange was interrupted by an angry shout. Mrs. Fitzpatrick stood at the gate. Sidney hadn't realized how much Bryan and his mother resembled each other until she saw Mrs. Fitzpatrick angry. Her hazel eyes flashed, and her eyebrows scrunched down low, almost lower than Bryan's.

"What on earth were you thinking, Bryan?" Mrs. Fitzpatrick said. "Get off that horse immediately."

Bryan scowled, but he slid off Magic's back. Magic calmed down almost as soon as Bryan hit the ground. Mrs. Fitzpatrick opened the gate and came in. She marched over and took Magic's reins.

"You are never to get on a horse, especially this horse, without me present. And without a helmet! Go on and get the helmets out of the tack room."

Bryan walked away sulkily, his shoulders drooping, while Jimmy chuckled at Bryan's expense. Sidney couldn't help but be amused. It was nice to see such a know-it-all get told off by his mother.

Mrs. Fitzpatrick took a deep breath and turned to the rest of her students. "I apologize for Bryan's behavior. Never get on a horse without asking me first and never, I mean *never*, get on a horse in my arena without a helmet."

She looked pointedly at Jimmy. "That means you, too."

Jimmy frowned. "But Western riders don't wear helmets. They wear cowboy hats."

Mrs. Fitzpatrick shook her head, her ponytail flying. "Not in my stables. If you want to ride here, you wear a helmet."

Jimmy removed his hat reluctantly.

"You can put it in the tack room for safekeeping," Mrs. Fitzpatrick said. "We don't want it blowing around and scaring the horses."

She took the bay horse's reins while Jimmy trotted off toward the tack room with his hat in hand.

A few minutes later, Jimmy returned wearing a helmet. While they waited on Bryan to return, Mrs. Fitzpatrick instructed the students on how to mount their horses.

"Why don't you show them, Jimmy?" she said.

Jimmy stood on the left side of his horse, gathered up his reins and swung himself easily onto Charlie's back. He shifted his weight in the saddle to make himself comfortable and patted Charlie on the neck.

"You make it look easy, Jimmy, but those stirrups look awfully high up," Jane said, surveying Misty's saddle.

"It'll be hard the first few times, but you'll get the hang of it," Jimmy said.

When Bryan returned, the girls strapped their helmets

on securely, and Mrs. Fitzpatrick told Bryan and the girls to mount their horses. Bryan jumped right back up onto Magic's back. Magic tried to start walking off before Bryan had gotten comfortable in the saddle, but the boy grabbed one rein and pulled the horse in a circle, bringing him to a stop.

Jane's face went red with embarrassment when she tried to heave herself up into the saddle and failed. She slid back down Misty's side and onto the ground. She looked around to see if anyone had noticed, but fortunately the boys were busy with their own mounts.

Mrs. Fitzpatrick came over and held Misty's reins. "Put your left foot in the stirrup," she said, "then bounce on your toes and spring up."

Jane followed her instructions and was able to clamber up awkwardly. Mrs. Fitzpatrick then did the same for Sidney.

Once she was on, Sidney settled into the saddle. It felt strange. When Jasper shifted his weight, the ground seemed to be moving beneath her. She grabbed his black mane for support, took a deep a breath, and looked around. It was the first time she'd seen the world from the back of a horse and she liked it.

CHAPTER 3

New Friends

"Shorten up on your reins, Sidney," Mrs. Fitzpatrick said. "If you let the reins get too loose, you'll lose control." The instructor stood in the middle of the arena with her hands on her hips while the riders circled slowly around her.

They had spent the last half hour or so working on the riding basics, like sitting properly in the saddle, steering the horse, and holding the reins correctly.

"Can we go faster yet?" Bryan whined. Magic looked eager to speed up as well. Bryan was able to keep him at a walk, but just barely. The horse's walk was choppy and every part of his tense body looked restrained and unhappy. Magic reminded Sidney of the racehorses she had seen on television a few weeks before. Those horses had been getting ready to race in the biggest race of all: the Kentucky Derby.

Jane glanced at Sidney as she rode up next to her. "Watching him ride that horse makes me nervous," she said. "It makes me appreciate Misty, even if she is a little sleepy."

Sidney nodded and patted Jasper on the neck. The big horse felt calm and collected beneath her. She felt safe on his broad back.

"I think we're ready to try a little trotting now," Mrs.

Fitzpatrick said. "I want you girls to watch Bryan and Jimmy first. Bring your horses to the center of the arena."

Sidney and Jane maneuvered their mounts to stand beside her in the middle of the oval arena.

"Now, watch how gentle they are with their horses," Mrs. Fitzpatrick said, gesturing toward Bryan and Jimmy. "Once you are at a walk, all you have to do is squeeze your legs to ask your horse to speed up. You never want to kick the horse."

"Trot!" Mrs. Fitzpatrick called. Bryan nodded and Magic immediately sprang into the faster gait. Jimmy followed right behind him on Charlie.

"It looks easy enough," Jane said, watching the boys ride around them.

"We just make it look easy," Bryan called to her with a smile. Magic looked much happier at trot and had calmed down enough for him to allow his attention to stray a bit.

"That's enough, Bryan," Mrs. Fitzpatrick said. She waved her hand, signaling for the boys to slow their horses. "Now, girls, you get out there and try it. Then we'll wrap up this lesson."

Sidney walked Jasper to the rail and followed it to the right. When she heard Mrs. Fitzpatrick call "Trot!" she squeezed her legs against Jasper's sides. The horse responded right away. The result surprised Sidney. The trot was so bumpy she felt like she might bounce right out of the saddle! She banged up and down on his back painfully, trying desperately to keep her balance. Grasping Jasper's black mane with one hand, she held anxiously onto the reins with the other, just trying to stay on.

"Calm down," Mrs. Fitzpatrick yelled. "It'll feel really different at first, but you'll get used to it. Just to try to go with the horse's rhythm."

Jasper followed the arena rail closely and by the time

he had circled the arena twice, Sidney felt a bit more comfortable and in control.

"Don't lean on the reins," Mrs. Fitzpatrick kept calling to her and Jane. "You'll hurt your horse's mouth."

Sidney managed to let go of his mane and hold the reins in both hands, but it took all the strength in her legs not to lean on them or use them for balance.

After only a few minutes, the reins felt slippery with sweat and her legs felt like jelly.

"Good," Mrs. Fitzpatrick said. "Now, sit deep in the saddle and pull back on the reins to slow the horse to a walk. Then bring your horse to a full stop."

Sidney followed her instructions. As soon as she pulled back gently, Jasper slowed to a walk. Holding the pressure on the bit, she continued to sit deeply in the saddle, and the horse came to a halt. Out of the corner of her eye, she saw Jane do the same with Misty on the other side of the arena.

"Perfect. Time to dismount."

* * *

"Now, we're going to untack the horses," Mrs. Fitzpatrick told the girls. Sidney saw Bryan roll his eyes and laugh quietly to himself. He had already led Magic into his stall, removed his bridle, and replaced it with a halter. Since there were only two crossties in the barn aisle, Mrs. Fitzpatrick had instructed the riders to tie the horses to the brass rings that hung in each of their stalls. Magic's stall was right across from Jasper's, and when she was sure Mrs. Fitzpatrick wasn't looking, Sidney made a face at Bryan. She was getting tired of his superior attitude. It was getting on her nerves. He responded by grinning back happily, which annoyed Sidney even more.

The boys, being more experienced riders, were done

caring for their horses long before Sidney and Jane. Jimmy left Charlie in a stall and came over to watch Sidney.

He had removed his helmet at the first opportunity and replaced it with his cowboy hat. It looked battered and old, like he wore it all the time.

"I like your hat," Sidney said.

Jimmy grinned. "Can I help you?" he asked, slipping into the stall. Even Sidney had to admit he was charming and sweet. The opposite of Bryan. "Then you'll be done twice as fast."

"Or even faster," Sidney joked. "You already finished caring for one horse faster than I could get started on mine!"

He laughed and picked up a brush from her grooming box. "That's not true. You've already untacked him."

Sidney rubbed Jasper in a rhythmic motion with the currycomb while she talked to Jimmy. Jasper seemed to like the attention. He leaned into the brush and closed his eyes, making Sidney giggle.

Jimmy followed behind her with the hard-bristled dandy brush, and in just a few minutes, what little dust Jasper had picked up in the arena had been removed from his coat. It shone just as brightly as before the ride.

Jimmy stepped back and leaned against the stall door while he watched her pick out Jasper's hooves with the hoof pick.

"Was this your first time riding?" he asked.

Sidney nodded. "Yep," she replied. "Besides the pony rides at the fair."

Jimmy shook his head and smiled. "I don't think those count."

"Probably not," Sidney agreed. She patted Jasper's neck and leaned in to whisper a thank you to him. He had been very well-behaved during the lesson, barely paying attention to Magic's antics.

She untied him from the brass ring and removed his halter, giving him one final pat before exiting the stall. Jimmy held the door open while she came out and closed and latched it carefully behind her.

"How long have you been riding?" Sidney asked, assessing him more closely. She had been so preoccupied with the horses during the lesson, she had hardly paid attention to her fellow students.

"A few years," Jimmy replied nonchalantly. "I started riding when I was about seven, I guess."

"How old are you now?"

"Almost twelve." He stuck his chest out and hooked his fingers through the belt loops on his worn jeans. Sidney almost laughed. He wore a long-sleeved button down shirt with a Western pattern that almost hurt her eyes to look at and a large shiny belt buckle. He looked like a tiny version of the bull riders she had seen on television.

A clatter from the other end of the barn aisle drew her attention away from Jimmy. Mrs. Fitzpatrick had removed the lid from a large canister and was handing out treats for the horses.

"Come and get them," Mrs. Fitzpatrick called down the aisle. Bryan and Jane had already collected treats and were headed back to their horses' stalls.

Sidney and Jimmy walked over together. She waited for Jimmy to take his, then held out her hand. Mrs. Fitzpatrick paused. "You did a wonderful job today, Sidney. I was very impressed."

"Thank you," Sidney replied, feeling a rush of happiness. "I had a great time. I can't wait for my next lesson."

Mrs. Fitzpatrick laughed and dropped a treat into Sidney's palm. "That's what I like to hear."

Sidney smiled and returned to Jasper's stall. He had his head hanging over the door, waiting. "You know what's coming, don't you, boy?" she said softly, holding the treat out for him.

Mrs. Fitzpatrick followed her over. "Hold your hand flat and put the treat on your palm. That way he can't accidentally bite your fingers."

Sidney did as she was told and Jasper picked the treat up off her palm with velvety lips. The treat didn't look appealing to Sidney. It was the color and texture of a dog treat, but it was shaped like a carrot. Jasper seemed to like it, though. He munched it noisily, slobber dripping from his mouth, and when he had finished he reached over to nudge Sidney's hand, looking for more.

She laughed and rubbed his nose. "No more today, Jasper. I've got to get back home. Mom'll be worried if I'm late. Besides, she'll want hear all about the lesson."

Just as Sidney and Jane were getting ready to leave, a tall man wearing a cowboy outfit very similar to Jimmy's walked into the barn.

He nodded to them and tipped his hat just the way Jimmy did. The girls waved back politely and held in their giggles until they had gotten out of his sight.

"That must be Jimmy's dad," Jane said as soon as they were out of the barn.

The pair walked slowly down the Fitzpatrick's long driveway and toward Jane's house.

"So, what did you think?" Sidney asked.

"About what?" Jane replied.

"The lesson? The horses?"

"It was fun," Jane replied, shrugging. "It seems like a lot of work, though. What do you think?"

"It does seem like a lot of work, but I loved it!" Sidney replied, her eyes shining. "I can't wait to ride Jasper again."

"Mrs. Fitzpatrick's nice," Jane said. "My mom likes her, so I figured she would be."

"Yes, your mom always likes the same people you do." Sidney rolled her eyes.

Jane smiled and wrinkled her nose. "She doesn't *dislike* you." She looped her arm through Sidney's.

"She just doesn't want us to be friends."

Jane shrugged. "She thinks you're a troublemaker."

She paused, glancing at Sidney guiltily.

"What is it?" Sidney asked. "You're not telling me something."

"I think she warned Mrs. Fitzpatrick about you."

Sidney frowned. "Warned her about me? I'm not a dangerous criminal."

Jane squeezed her arm lightly. "Of course not. She just told her to watch out for you. You might cause trouble."

Sidney sighed deeply, a wounded look on her face. "What do I have to do to convince her I'm not going to get into any trouble this summer?"

"She'll believe it when she sees it," Jane replied.

"We did dig up all her flowers last summer," Jane added. "She was very upset about that. And remember the summer before that when we tried to paint the house for her and Dad? We thought we were doing them a favor."

"How could we have known she wouldn't like her house to be hot pink?" Sidney laughed. "How did we get that paint anyway?"

"She was going to paint our clubhouse for us," Jane said. "She bought that paint and left it in the shed because she hadn't gotten around to it yet."

"Well, we were children then. I was eight that summer! We're practically grown up now."

When they reached the bottom of the driveway, Sidney paused. "Shouldn't we have put our tack away?"

A saddle stand was set outside of each stall for the riders to use while tacking and untacking. The girls had both left their tack there instead of returning it to the tack room.

Jane stopped quickly, skidding a little on the loose gravel in the drive. "Oops. She did say we were supposed take it back to tack room after every ride... and sometimes even clean it."

"She'll have to put it all back by herself if we don't do it."

Jane glanced back toward the barn. "I guess we can go back and help. It would only take a few minutes."

They retraced their steps and found Mrs. Fitzpatrick standing just outside the barn talking to Jimmy's father.

She glanced at them curiously as they approached. "We didn't put our tack back in the tack room," Sidney explained.

Mrs. Fitzpatrick nodded and smiled. "I would've taken care of it for you this time, but it was sweet of you to come back."

Jimmy's father grinned at the girls. "You've got some dedicated students, Cindy." Messy blond hair stuck out at odd angles from under his cowboy hat. He looked so much like Jimmy it was almost creepy. It was like seeing a future version of the boy.

"Jimmy's still in there. Get him to help you put your stuff away." He winked at the girls, and they exchanged glances.

"Thank you, sir," Sidney said politely, nodding at the man.

The girls found Jimmy outside Charlie's stall. Charlie had his head over the half door, and Jimmy was scratching between the horse's ears.

"My dad's talking to Mrs. Fitzpatrick about boarding Charlie at Blue Moon. That way we won't have to haul him here every week for lessons."

"That'll be great!" Sidney said. She reached out and rubbed Charlie's forehead gently. He closed his eyes just like Jasper had done.

"What are you doing back? I thought you left," A whiny voice said.

Sidney turned around to see Bryan standing behind them. "We forgot to put our tack up."

"I haven't put mine up yet either," Jimmy said. "I got distracted."

Bryan frowned and glanced over at his own. His tack was piled in a heap outside his stall door. He hadn't even bothered to use the saddle rack.

"Well, I guess we better," Bryan sighed.

The four riders gathered their saddles and other gear up and carried it all toward the tack room. Jimmy reached the door first. It creaked when he pulled it open.

"Jimmy," Jane groaned from behind him. "Can you go on in? This saddle is heavy and you're blocking the door."

He stood stock still in the doorframe, shielding the tack room from view.

"Jimmy?" she said again. She nudged him in the back with her elbow. He finally edged into the room.

"Oh no!" Jane cried when she finally managed to get inside.

"What is it?" Sidney said. At the tail end of the group, all she could see was the back of Bryan's head.

"Someone's wrecked the tack room," Jimmy stammered. "A lot of stuff is ruined."

"What!" Bryan yelled. He tossed his armful of tack to the ground and pushed past Jane roughly.

"Who did this?" He turned on the other three riders.

Jimmy stepped over piles of halters, saddles, blankets, and various other horse supplies and set his saddle carefully on an empty saddle rack. "Don't look at us, Bryan. Why would we want to do this?"

The floor was so littered with fallen or thrown objects it was difficult to even walk across the room. Jimmy got tangled in a halter and almost fell on his way back to the door. Sidney sighed deeply as she looked around. Jane put a hand up to her nose. "What's that smell?"

Jimmy bent down and picked up an empty bottle. A little yellow liquid dribbled out. "Neatsfoot oil. It's used on the leather."

"Who could do such a thing?" Jane cringed away from the scene. "Poor Mrs. Fitzpatrick. Whoever did it must be a monster to do this to such a nice lady."

Bryan looked livid. "I told my mother we should never have come here! This place is cursed. It's been nothing but trouble," he yelled. He stood shaking and silent for a second, staring at the other riders, then stomped out, leaving his tack on the floor outside the tack room door.

Mrs. Fitzpatrick came in a few seconds later with tears in her eyes. Jimmy's father followed just behind her.

"Gadzooks," Jimmy's father whistled. "Someone sure made a mess."

The three students stood transfixed. Bryan didn't return.

"I'm so sorry, Mrs. Fitzpatrick," Jane said. "This is terrible."

Mrs. Fitzpatrick shook her head and sighed. "Go on home, girls," she replied, crestfallen. Her shoulders slumped forward in a defeated sort of way and wrinkles creased her forehead.

Sidney and Jane stared at her. It didn't feel right to just leave.

Jimmy's father nodded at Sidney and Jane. "She's right. You girls go on home. Jimmy and I will help her clean this up, won't we, Jim?"

Jimmy nodded and his father patted him on the back. "We'll have it ship-shape again in no time, Mrs. Fitzpatrick," Jimmy replied encouragingly.

The girls looked at each other and walked reluctantly from the ruined tack room.

CHAPTER 4

The Old Barn

Sidney and Jane climbed wearily up the porch steps of the Abbots' home, collapsing into the two wooden chairs by the front door.

"That was just terrible," Sidney said. Jane looked distressed as well, and Sidney reached out to take her hand.

"I feel like we should we do something," Sidney continued. Jane nodded, her face pinched and worried.

Jane seemed spoiled to Sidney sometimes and would throw the occasional fit when fighting with her mother, but Sidney knew she hated confrontation and usually avoided it if she could. The tack room incident seemed to have really bothered her.

"But what can we do?" Jane said, her eyes wide. "It wasn't either of us. It must have been Jimmy or Bryan. Mrs. Fitzpatrick must know that."

Sidney shrugged and rubbed her sweaty face with a dirty hand, leaving a streak of brown on her cheek. "I don't know. Can we say that for sure? Anyone could've snuck in and trashed the tack room while we were all out in the arena for the lesson. And we weren't exactly keeping tabs on each other while we were all untacking and grooming our horses. I wouldn't have noticed if someone left their horse's stall for five minutes. That's all it would take. Any of us could've done it."

"That's true, I guess."

"Bryan acted like this wasn't the first strange thing that's happened. He said the place is cursed."

"Curses aren't real, Sid."

"I know that," Sidney scoffed. She kicked a pebble off the porch with the toe of her boot and looked thoughtfully at the ground. "The question is *why*. Mrs. Fitzpatrick must have an enemy. Someone who wants to upset her."

The front door opened and Mrs. Abbot peered out. "Hi, girls. How was the lesson?"

"Mom –" Jane started, but her mother interrupted her.

"You need to come in and shower, Jane, and get ready for your dance lesson tonight. Ballet, I think."

"But, Mom – "

"Now, Jane. If you're not in that shower in ten minutes, I'll be back out to get you." Mrs. Fitzpatrick disappeared back inside the house and the door slammed shut.

Jane rolled her eyes and smiled at Sidney. "I guess I better go."

She stood up and, pausing with her hand on the doorknob, she tilted her head to the side and looked at Sidney slyly. "What were you talking about with Jimmy for so long?"

"Nothing important. He said he's been riding for years. He seems nice, but a little arrogant."

Jane smiled, batting her pale blue eyes comically. "Maybe he likes you."

Sidney shook her head. "I doubt it. He seems to like himself a lot, though."

The pair laughed.

"Well, while you were talking to Jimmy, I was talking

to Bryan," Jane said. She let go of the doorknob and leaned against the door instead. She reached up and released her blonde hair from its ponytail. The new haircut made her look older. Her long locks had been chopped off and replaced with short layers. It now hung only to her shoulders, framing her face prettily.

"What did he have to say? He never says anything nice from what I've seen," Sidney said.

"He's not that bad. Actually...."

Jane fiddled with her hair and looked away.

"Actually what?"

"I might have invited him to come play with us tomorrow. I said we could go exploring."

"With Bryan?" Sidney exclaimed.

"Yes, with Bryan." Jane put her hands on her hips. "Don't you remember when you first moved here?"

Sidney nodded slowly, not liking where this was going.

"It was during the summer and school was out. I met you right over there." Jane pointed to her front yard. "I invited you to come play with me. Didn't that make you happy?"

Sidney nodded reluctantly. "But I wasn't like Bryan."

"Give him a chance, Sid. He's a nice kid. He's just upset about moving. He had to leave all his friends behind."

Sidney groaned. "Fine. He can play with us tomorrow."

She put a lot of emphasis on the word tomorrow, and Jane looked at her with narrowed eyes. Then she smiled. "Thanks, Sid. He just seems so unhappy."

* * *

The next day, Bryan came over just after lunchtime.

Sidney and Jane were sitting on the front steps of Sidney's house waiting for him.

He moseyed over, looking around the yard, and greeted them with forced cheer when he got close enough.

"Let's go play in the backyard," Jane suggested quickly. "Sidney has an awesome tire swing."

Bryan agreed and the three walked slowly around the house.

"What's with the walk?" Bryan asked, looking doubtfully at Sidney's and Jane's legs.

Jane made a face and glanced at Sidney. "We didn't know riding would make us so sore!"

Bryan snickered.

"Sorry," he said, when he saw the pained look on their faces. "You'll be sore for a while. At least until your legs get used to riding a horse instead of walking."

Jane hopped into the tire swing and Sidney grabbed it and ran in circles. She let go and laughed while Jane spun around and squealed. Bryan was next. He put his legs through the hole in the center of the tire reluctantly.

"Not too fast," he said. Jane grabbed the tire this time, but she didn't run quite as many circles as Sidney had. Bryan didn't spin around nearly as fast as Jane, but when he came to a stop, Sidney was happy to see he was grinning ear-to-ear.

They played on the swing for almost half an hour, only stopping when Sidney's mother came out to say hello, offering them lemonade and cookies. They accepted and went inside reluctantly. The sun had grown so bright and the air so mild and fresh they didn't want to return indoors.

Bryan seemed somewhat cheerful. Mrs. Sinclair asked him several questions and he answered all of them with a smile. He seemed like a different Bryan today. Surely this couldn't be the boy Sidney met at Blue Moon Stables? He'd been rude to his own mother and acted like a brat. This boy seemed eager to please and even polite.

"Bryan might be in one of your classes. Right, Mom?" Sidney said. She looked up at her mother with admiration.

Mrs. Sinclair nodded and set a plate of sweet treats on the table along with an ice-cold pitcher of lemonade.

"I hope so. It'd be nice to know a few people," Bryan said.

Mrs. Sinclair sat down next to Bryan and offered him a cookie. Being a teacher, Sidney's mother was great with young people and had Bryan opening up to her in just minutes. He even talked a little bit about his old school and friends. His eyes lit up when he talked about them, and Sidney could see how much it was hurting him to be away from them.

He seemed to be enjoying himself right up until Sidney mentioned the tack room incident, then he clammed up. "I don't want to talk about it," he said. "Mom still doesn't know who did it and she's really upset."

Sidney started to argue that the three of them should figure out who did it together. If they solved the case, Mrs. Fitzpatrick wouldn't have to be upset and worried anymore. But Jane shook her head warningly and Sidney snapped her mouth shut, silently vowing not to discuss the matter further, even though she wanted to badly. Bryan had finally started acting like he was having some fun and she didn't want to be the one to ruin it.

"Where are we going to explore?" Bryan asked, sitting on the edge of his chair at the kitchen table. He had finished his lemonade quickly and was taking small bites of a chocolate chip cookie to make up for it. Sidney's mom poured some more lemonade into his glass with a smile.

Sidney and Jane looked at each other.

"There's an old barn behind my house," Jane offered. "We could take Snapper and Sam with us."

Mrs. Sinclair put a warning hand on Sidney's shoulder. "You be careful. You can go around the barn, but don't go inside. Old buildings can be dangerous."

Sidney nodded. Her mother had said so a thousand times. She and Jane had never gone in and always kept a safe distance. The barn looked like a small gust of wind could bring it down.

"Who are Snapper and Sam?" Bryan asked, wiping his mouth. He had drained his second glass of lemonade with amazing speed.

"My dogs," Jane responded proudly. "They're German shepherds."

"Wow! I've always wanted a dog," Bryan said with envy. He looked genuinely excited. He smiled at Sidney and, for the first time, she thought they could actually be friends.

* * *

After collecting Snapper and Sam from Jane's backyard, the threesome threaded their way through the weedy tree line that ran behind the girls' houses.

"Cool," Bryan said, picking up a long stick to slash at the vegetation.

"It's this way." Sidney pushed a branch back with one hand while she ducked under another larger one.

"It's like a jungle in here," Jane said, laughing. She scoured the ground until she found a long stick similar to Bryan's. She pointed it at him and took a swordfighter stance. "En garde," she said, waving the stick comically.

Bryan laughed and jumped into a fighting stance as

well. "Are you sure about this? I think I can take you."

Jane wiggled her eyebrows and snarled. "Do you? Then you don't know that I am the most fearsome swordfighter the world has ever seen."

Sidney stopped to wait on them, tapping her foot. She didn't appreciate a game only two could play at. "Any day now!"

Snapper and Sam had already bounded ahead and disappeared between the trees.

Jane and Bryan began weaving among the trunks, batting their sticks at each other and only occasionally hitting the mark. They laughed and ducked simultaneously, following Sidney but paying more attention to each other.

Sidney stomped hard on a thorn bush. "Snapper! Sam!" she called. She couldn't hear the dogs anymore, and Jane usually didn't like it when they got too far away.

She tramped on. Soon the trees thinned out and the barn came into view. It sat alone in a large field. It belonged to an older man, a farmer. Since he'd become ill, he'd retired from farming and left the barn to elements. The barn was already old then, and now it looked ancient.

Its gray wooden sides were weathered and overgrown with weeds and vines, and the tin roof was a rusty red-brown color. The middle of the barn sagged sadly. Numerous animals lived inside but not the animals the barn was meant to house. It was largely populated with mice and other small vermin. The mice were enough to keep Sidney and Jane out, but they weren't the only residents. A few birds had built their homes there as well. They flew in and out of holes in the roof. And, once or twice, the girls had even spotted a stray cat or a fox slipping in or out of the barn.

"Here it is," Sidney said with satisfaction. She stopped and put her hands on her hips. "And there you are," she added. Snapper and Sam played and rolled in the tall grass a few feet in front of the threesome.

Sidney and Jane had discovered the barn a year ago on one of their treks through the woods. They liked to pack up picnic lunches and take them to the barn. They usually sat in the soft grass under the trees and ate, admiring it safely from afar.

As Jane had said last summer, "The barn looks lonely, and we must go to keep it company for a while."

Bryan's eyes widened as he gazed at the old building, and he let out a long, low whistle, which Sidney admired very much. She had been trying to learn to whistle in vain for the last several months. She decided to ask him later if he could teach her.

"Isn't it great?" Jane said, tossing her hair behind her shoulder casually. "Sidney and I found it together. It's our secret hangout."

"It isn't very secret if your mother knows about it," Bryan responded quickly.

Jane looked annoyed but merely shrugged and walked over to where Sidney stood. Bryan made as if to follow her, and then changed his mind. With a glance in their direction, he headed directly toward the barn.

"Have you been inside?" he asked, approaching the side of the barn cautiously.

"Of course not," Jane replied. "You heard Mrs. Sinclair. It could be dangerous in there. Besides, there are spiders and mice."

She shivered and made a face. Jane had a deathly fear of spiders. She had a fear of all bugs, but spiders especially.

"Well, I'm not scared," Bryan sneered. He placed a

hand on the side of the old barn and turned to look at them. "It seems pretty solid."

Sidney frowned. "You should get away from there. Jane and I always stay over here in the grass. That way if anything falls, it won't fall on us."

Bryan laughed and pounded his palm against the old wood. Dust flew up from under his hand, and he sneezed.

Jane giggled, but quickly stopped when she saw the look on Sidney's face.

"Bryan!" Sidney shouted. "Stop that right now!"

Sidney stomped her booted foot on the ground and clenched her fists. The nerve of him! He thought he could just waltz into her and Jane's place and ignore the rules. He was trying to take over their place for himself.

Suddenly, a horrible thought came to Sidney. What if Jane liked bold, adventurous Bryan better than her? In her mind's eye, Sidney saw Bryan and Jane coming to this place on their own, having picnics right where Jane stood now, keeping the barn company. They would have sword fights with sticks and laugh and play without her.

The vision vanished almost as soon as it had come, but the anger didn't. Sidney stomped her foot again and screamed, "Bryan!"

Bryan wiped the dust from his face and held his hands up. "All right, all right. Calm down. I stopped."

"Come back over here," Jane said coaxingly, taking a seat on the ground. She shot a warning glance at Sidney, her blue eyes disapproving.

Sidney frowned and sat down nearby, stretching her legs out in front of her.

Bryan slouched over to the pair and sunk down next to Jane. The dogs followed suit, tired of their games.

"You didn't have to over-react like that," Bryan said,

eyeing Sidney strangely with his thick brows lowered. "I wasn't going to get killed or anything. I can look after myself."

Sidney leaned back on her elbows and looked up at the sky. Only a few clouds littered the vast sea of blue above her. She sighed, letting the anger drain away. The thought of Jane choosing Bryan over her had upset her. But surely it was a silly idea. She didn't know what put it into her head. Their friendship was solid. They cared too much about one another to let such a surly boy get in the way. And how could she be in a bad mood on such a beautiful May day?

"I'm sure you can," she responded, not looking at him.

He continued to stare at Sidney for a long time, but Sidney refused to return his gaze. Jane finally distracted him with a game of tic-tac-toe, which she drew with her finger in the dirt.

After about fifteen minutes, Bryan sighed. He had lost his third game of tic-tac-toe in a row.

"What's the matter? Tired of losing?" Jane asked teasingly.

Bryan scowled and got up, stretching his arms over his head. He glanced at Sidney. She was flat out on the ground staring determinedly at the sky, her red hair fanned out behind her.

He whistled a quick tune, watching her closely. Her eyes darted to his face and then closed quickly. He stopped whistling abruptly and turned away.

"Bryan," Jane said, getting up from the ground and brushing the dirt from her pants. "Why don't we go back? I'm getting kind of thirsty. It's getting hot out here."

Bryan didn't respond. He started walking toward the old barn with long, determined strides.

"Bryan?" Jane said, confused. Her voice always

warbled slightly when she was nervous, and it did so now. Sidney opened her eyes and sat up, unable to ignore it.

"What's he doing?" Sidney asked Jane, looking up at her.

Jane shrugged and tugged at her blonde hair in agitation. The sun gleamed off the golden strands, and her blue eyes, wide with worry, were framed with long dark lashes. They looked like they had makeup on them, even though Sidney knew they did not.

"Bryan," Jane said again, her voice a little higher than before, "come on. Let's go home."

Bryan didn't turn around.

Sidney clambered up from the ground, wiping dirt vigorously from her pants and back. "Bryan!"

She yelled his name urgently, but he stomped forward, not even glancing back at the two girls, and went right up to the barn's two front doors. They were hanging off the hinges, one of them only propped up against the wall. He slipped into the darkness between them and disappeared.

Jane fell silent, her mouth hanging open, and Sidney went over and took her hand.

"He actually went in there," Sidney said in a hushed whisper.

Jane nodded, blinking rapidly. During their picnics, the two had often discussed what was inside the old barn. Aside from the commonplace, like the mice and spiders, they had come up with a variety of fantastical contents that could be waiting inside for someone to find them. Glittering jewels. A long forgotten chest filled with gold. A skeleton.

Despite all the stories they'd made up, they'd never been tempted to go in and look for themselves. Aside from the obvious danger, it would have ruined the fun. If they went in and found nothing, their stories would skid to a halt right then. They could no longer speculate on the contents of the building.

After the first shock of seeing their barn, the barn they had come to call their own, violated by Bryan, they ran forward. Sidney slid to a halt about ten feet from the barn door. Inside, she could only see darkness with a patch of light here and there on the floor where the sun shone in through holes in the ceiling.

"Bryan?" Sidney ventured, edging forward cautiously. She stopped just outside the door with Jane on her heels.

"Bryan?" Jane called, her voice quiet and low. Their reverence for the barn kept them from yelling too loudly.

No answer. A faint creaking of wood came from within but nothing else.

Sidney looked to Jane, and Jane looked to Sidney. Neither knew what to do. They were forbidden to enter the barn, but what had become of Bryan? He could have fallen and hurt himself. He could need their help.

Sidney took a deep breath and steeled herself before edging as close as she dared to the gaping opening through which Bryan had disappeared.

Suddenly, a noise came from out of the dark in front of them: a loud screech. They both jumped back a step. Sidney's heart beat so hard it hurt, and she felt sick to her stomach. She couldn't see anything in the darkness within.

"What was it?" Jane whispered. She was choking on tears, and her words came out garbled.

"I don't know," Sidney whispered back. Her muscles felt tense. She wanted to run, but she didn't. She stood her ground and listened closely. She heard something just in front of them, a faint scratching, but she couldn't see anything. She reached forward, searching with her hands, and hit something. It grabbed her arm and pushed her backwards.

"Whoa!" Sidney yelled, falling heavily into Jane, who tripped backward and landed on the ground on her behind. Sidney landed in her lap. The two struggled to get up, but they were tangled up with each other and the underbrush. While they were still struggling, Bryan emerged, laughing, from the barn.

"Thought you could ignore me, did you?" Bryan said grinning at Sidney. He offered her a hand up from the ground, but she didn't accept. She pulled herself up on her own and stood in front of him angrily, trying to ignore the pain from a scrape on her leg.

"What on earth is wrong with you?" she said. Tears came to her eyes, but she blinked them away.

Jane flailed on the ground, struggling to get up, but she was tangled up in the thick growing weeds. She jerked at her ankle, trying desperately to remove herself from the snarl of underbrush.

Bryan brushed past Sidney and bent down to next to Jane. He put a hand on her shoulder to still her. "Hey. Stop moving. I'll cut you loose." He pulled a pocketknife from his back pocket and cut at the tangle of underbrush until the weeds fell away and released her.

She wouldn't look at him, which made Sidney happy, but she did allow him to help her up. He looked genuinely upset about her anger and apologized several times.

"I didn't mean to push you so hard," he said pleadingly. "I didn't know you would trip."

The two girls ignored his pleas for forgiveness completely and hugged each other. Jane checked Sidney's scraped leg and assured her that it didn't look too bad, and Sidney glared at Bryan when he offered to bandage it for her with his shirt.

Their adventure had turned sour, and all three knew it was over. In single file, they headed back toward the woods, leaving the old barn to its lonely field.

* * *

The trip back to Sidney's house was a quiet one. Snapper and Sam ran ahead as usual, their spirits not dampened by the heated exchange between the humans they didn't understand.

The threesome tramped through the trees behind the two playful dogs at a fast pace. There was little talking. After several attempts at apologizing with no response, Bryan gave up.

They reached Sidney's house quickly and Bryan, his face red and sweaty, apologized one more time. When he got no response, he looked miserably from Jane to Sidney and lowered his gaze to the ground.

"I guess I'll see you guys at the riding lesson next week," he said.

Jane and Sidney watched while he turned and walked slowly across the lawn toward the road.

Jane sighed and rubbed the back of her neck. Her hair was mussed and pieces of leaves still clung to some strands. "I almost feel sorry for him."

Sidney frowned. "I don't. He pushed us down. I haven't been pushed down since kindergarten."

They sat down on the front porch steps, watching Snapper and Sam play in the yard. Mrs. Sinclair came out and sat behind them in the porch swing, a large glass of iced tea in her hand.

"How did your exploration go?" she asked, sipping delicately from her glass.

Jane turned to look at her. "Not well."

Sidney's mother looked at Jane's hair with raised

eyebrows and sighed. "I see. No one got hurt?"

Sidney shook her head. "No," she replied, even though the long scratch on her leg still smarted.

"Good," Sidney's mother said. "It's nice of you to invite Bryan over. His mother's worried about him. School isn't in and it's hard to make friends in a new town. You can understand that, Sid."

Sidney rolled her eyes, but her mother didn't see. "I know, Mom."

"Well, try to get along with him. Try to be nice," she replied.

"*We* are nice," Sidney said, picking a leaf out Jane's hair and throwing it to the ground.

Sidney's mother smiled. "I know you are, Sid. Once school starts, he'll find other friends. Just try to include him until then."

Sidney sighed and looked at Jane despondently, "We will."

CHAPTER 5

Livestock At Large

Sidney woke up the next morning to an odd sound beneath her window. She rolled over in bed, pulling the covers up to her chin, and tried to ignore it, but it wouldn't go away.

She squinted at the clock on her bedside table. Five o'clock in the morning.

The sound faded. Sidney groaned and closed her eyes. It was probably her imagination. Or maybe Snapper and Sam had gotten loose again. Sometimes they dug under the fence, and when they escaped they usually made a mess, knocking over flowerpots and jumping in and out of the porch swing. The two dogs seemed to delight in playing in the Sinclairs' yard because it wasn't theirs.

Oh, well. They can wait to be put up for a few more hours, Sidney thought, *it's almost morning.*

She was just drifting off to sleep when she heard the sound again. This time she was awake enough to realize what it was: not Snapper and Sam, but hoofbeats. A horse!

She shot out of bed and immediately tripped over her boots, which she had discarded beside her bed instead of putting in the closet like she was supposed to do.

She was sent reeling and ended up sprawled over the

plush chair by her bedroom window.

Sidney groaned and rubbed her big toe, which she had banged against the hard tip of her riding boot. Grabbing her bookcase for support, she pulled herself upright. It was difficult to see anything in the oppressive darkness of the room. Usually the moon provided some light, but not tonight. *It must be cloudy out there*, she thought.

She peered out the window, craning her neck to see all areas of the yard. It was so shadowy, though, it was impossible to see much. A raindrop splattered against the glass pane. Another followed just behind it, then another, and another. They began pattering softly against the window in a rhythmic fashion.

"Great," Sidney whispered. She discarded her pajama bottoms and put on an old pair of jeans. She pulled on the offending boots without even putting on socks and opened her bedroom door slowly. It creaked softly but not loudly enough to wake her mother.

She eased down the stairs, avoiding the places she knew from experience creaked the loudest. In that way, she made it to the front door. She retrieved a flashlight from a drawer in the front hallway and unlocked the door as quietly as she could. She didn't want her mother to think someone was breaking in.

She stuck her head out into the darkness and heard the sound again. It was the drumming of hoofbeats, except it was now accompanied by the whispering sound of softly falling rain. Sidney stepped out onto the porch and turned on the flashlight, shining it all around the yard.

There! She stopped just where her yard met the Abbots' yard. A horse whose black coat had made him almost invisible in the darkness lifted his head from the Abbots' carefully mown grass and looked at her.

"Jasper!" Sidney said loudly. He pricked his ears

forward and took a step in her direction.

She approached him slowly, afraid she would scare him away. He didn't move. He munched his mouthful of grass calmly and watched her come closer. When she got close enough, he nudged her hand with his nose, looking for a treat.

Sidney giggled and ran a hand down the white stripe on his face. "No treats tonight, buddy."

Now what to do? She didn't have anything to tie him up with or to lead him back home. *I need a rope*, Sidney thought, looking around.

No, I need Jane. She frowned. Even if she had a rope to lead Jasper with, she didn't want to walk all the way up Mrs. Fitzgerald's long driveway with just Jasper for company. Not on a dark, rainy night.

"You stay here, boy," Sidney said, patting Jasper on the neck. She couldn't just go into the Abbots' house. And she didn't want to wake Mrs. Abbot. *Nope, I don't want to wake the dragon*, she thought, giggling. Mrs. Abbot would probably blame Jasper's escape on Sidney!

She made her way around the house to the backyard and slipped in through the gate.

Sam let out a loud bark. "Shhh!" Sidney held a finger up to her lips and glared at the big dog. He wagged his tail and walked over to lick her hand. Sidney took that as an apology and patted him on the head. She looked at the windows to make sure no lights had come on. Jane's bedroom was on the second floor like Sidney's but it looked out over the backyard instead of the front. All the windows were still dark, including Jane's.

"Okay, Sam," Sidney said. "We have to wake Jane up."

She shivered. The rain was barely coming down. Only a few droplets clung to her hair and a few more had dotted her T-shirt with wet spots, but the night had grown quite chilly.

She looked around on the ground until she found a small stone. It was too small to break the glass. She hoped it was anyway. She aimed it at the window and let it fly, but it fell several feet short, bouncing off the side of the house.

She found another and did the same thing. This time the pebble hit its target and made a small ting! against the glass.

Sidney continued throwing pebbles in this way for about ten minutes with no response. Snapper looked at her quizzically as she threw the last stone. "Well," Sidney told the dog, "it was worth a try. It always works in the movies."

Sidney searched around the yard for something else to throw. Her eyes lighted on the pool shed. The door opened easily and almost noiselessly on well-oiled hinges. Inside, Sidney found a variety of pool tools and toys stacked on shelves and leaning against the wall. She rummaged around looking at different items and gauging their effectiveness in reaching the window.

Just as she was about to exit the shed with a handful of pool toys, she saw the pool cleaner Mr. Abbot used to clean leaves and other debris from the pool. The long, extendable stick would reach the window. She was sure of it. She wouldn't even have to throw anything.

She laughed aloud and returned the items she had been carrying to their places. "This is perfect!" she said to Sam, who had followed her in.

She herded Sam out and closed the door, carrying the pool cleaner with her. She positioned herself just under Jane's window and extended the stick to its fullest. It reached, but just barely.

She knocked against the window rhythmically. It was

just like knocking on a door, only she had to be very careful not to be too loud about it. After a few minutes, Jane's face appeared between the window curtains.

She looked confused and opened the window a crack. "Sidney?" she whispered. Sidney barely heard her voice over the patter of rain on the concrete pool deck. It was beginning to pick up.

Cool droplets pelted Sidney's forehead as she looked up at her friend. "Come down, Jane! I need to talk to you. Bring a rope!"

She whispered this urgently, and Jane did not question it for a moment, though she did look at Sidney like she might have lost her mind. Sidney gestured that she would meet her around front and went over to the gate. She left the pool cleaner leaned against the fence and, giving each dog a final pat on the head, let herself out and went back around to the front yard. Jasper was still grazing nonchalantly.

Jane came out onto the porch, two dog leashes in hand, to find Sidney leaning against the black horse, a small flashlight in her hand and wide grin on her face.

"What on earth?" Jane covered her mouth. She wore a soft pink robe and white slippers. Not exactly appropriate for walking Jasper back home.

"It's Jasper," Sidney whispered. Jane tossed one of the leashes down to Sidney, who caught it neatly. She wrapped it around Jasper's neck and stood awkwardly beside him, unsure of what to do next.

"I know who it is," said Jane, putting her hands on her hips, the other dog leash still dangling from her fingers. "How did he get here?"

Sidney shrugged. "I don't know. I woke up and heard him running outside my window."

Jane came down from the porch and rubbed his

shoulder. It felt cool and dry save for a few wet streaks from raindrops. "Are you sure it was him? He isn't breathing hard or anything. He's not sweaty. He doesn't look like he's been running at all."

Sidney paused and looked at the horse. He surveyed her with large brown eyes without a flicker of worry or excitement in them. "You're right. He seems very calm."

Jane looked around, but besides the light from the flashlight, it was very dark. The shrubs and trees looked like dark blobs. If there was another horse out there, it would be difficult to spot.

"Should we take him back and wake up Mrs. Fitzgerald?" Sidney asked hesitantly. She hadn't even thought seriously about waking an adult. In fact, she had actively tried *not* to wake an adult. She had wanted to solve the problem all her own and now she felt silly. If one horse was loose, the others could be as well.

"Maybe I should wake my parents," Jane suggested. "They'll be mad if I go walking around in the middle of the night."

"Okay," Sidney whispered. She glanced back toward her house doubtfully. She'd rather wake her own mother.

"I'll be right back," Jane said. She disappeared through the front door, closing it softly behind her. Sidney waited impatiently at the foot of the front steps holding Jasper by the dog lead. The horse pulled his head down and nibbled the grass. She tried to force his head back up, but he was much too determined to get at the well-kept lawn.

"You're so strong, Jasper." She gasped for breath and yanked on the dog leash. He ignored her and continued ripping up the neatly cut green blades with his teeth.

Jane finally reappeared with Mrs. Abbot on her heels. Mrs. Abbot sighed dramatically and put her hand on her chest when she saw Jasper eating her yard.

"Sorry, Mom," Jane said, looking up at her apologetically.

"It's not your fault, dear," Mrs. Abbot replied dolefully. She came hesitantly down the steps and stood in front of Jasper and Sidney.

"Well, I guess we need to get this horse back home," Mrs. Abbot said. "I'll just call Cindy and get her to come pick him up. It's far too dangerous for you girls to walk him across the road, especially without the proper equipment. Is that Sam's lead, Jane?"

Jane nodded and ducked her head. Mrs. Abbot frowned and went back indoors.

"I hope none of the others are loose," Jane said.

Mrs. Abbot returned a minute later. "She'll be here momentarily. Until then, take him over to your yard, Sidney. Your parent's lawn could use a trim anyway."

Mrs. Abbot sat primly on the edge of the nearest porch chair.

Sidney led Jasper over to her own yard and stood uncomfortably by him while he grazed. The morning dew and the rain had made the grass wet and the ankles of her jeans clung to her skin with moisture. Her shirt was beginning to feel uncomfortably damp as well. She was on her way to being thoroughly soaked. Goose bumps formed up and down her forearms.

Jane made a sympathetic face but instead of coming down off the porch to join Sidney, she sat near her mother on the other porch chair.

Sidney didn't blame her. There was no point in both of them getting wet.

"There. Her lights are coming on," Mrs. Abbot said with relief. "She'll be here in no time."

Sidney followed her gaze. Across the road, the Fitzpatricks' house and barn lights had come to life and shone brightly in the dark.

Poor Mrs. Fitzpatrick, Sidney thought, *first the tack room disaster and now this. Could it be...?*

Sidney shook her head vigorously to get the thought out of her mind. She knew what Jane would say. She was being silly. *Curses aren't real, Sid.*

Well, Jane was right, as usual. A tree had probably fallen on the pasture fence or someone had left a gate unlatched.

Only five minutes later, Mrs. Fitzpatrick pulled up in her blue pickup truck. To Sidney's dismay, she had Bryan with her. He hopped out first and ran over to Sidney, carrying a halter and lead in his hand. He helped her put it on Jasper.

"I'll take him home," Bryan told his mother. She nodded but looked over the horse first to make sure he hadn't sustained any injuries.

"Thank you so much for catching him and calling me," Mrs. Fitzpatrick said to Mrs. Abbot. Mrs. Abbot smiled and started to say something, but Jane suddenly piped up, "It was Sidney who caught him, Mrs. Fitzpatrick. She saw him and woke us up."

"Is that right?" Mrs. Fitzpatrick turned to thank Sidney. She put a hand on her shoulder and bent down to look her in the eye. "I'm impressed. You did the right thing, Sidney."

Sidney blushed and looked down at her feet.

"Is Jasper the only one that escaped, Mrs. Fitzpatrick? I thought I heard a horse running, but I don't think it was him."

Mrs. Fitzpatrick frowned. "You're right, Sidney. I had put Jasper and Magic out to pasture together, so Magic is out here somewhere, too. I hope we find him quickly. He's much spookier than Jasper and might get himself hurt."

"Magic was in there!" Bryan almost dropped Jasper's lead. His face lost all its coloring. "I saw him after supper and he was in his stall."

"I put him out in the pasture when I went out to check on everything before I went to bed. He looked antsy in his stall."

Bryan looked close to tears.

"Don't worry. We'll find him," his mother said. "You go ahead and take Jasper home."

"I'll help you look," Sidney replied. "I think Magic's close because I heard him running. That's how I found Jasper. It woke me up."

"Well, you better wake your mom and ask her first," Mrs. Fitzpatrick replied. "Just look in your backyard for me if you will. I don't want to go on your parent's property without permission."

"They won't mind," Sidney said but she ran off to look in the backyard for the missing horse.

Bryan walked off leading Jasper, and Mrs. Abbot and Jane went back inside, promising to keep a look out for Magic and to call if they saw anything.

* * *

Two hours later, Sidney was soaked to the bone and exhausted. Her mother looked almost as bedraggled as she did. After waking her mother, the pair had gone to help Mrs. Fitzpatrick search for Magic.

"I'm glad he wasn't hurt badly," Sidney said as she struggled out of her wet jacket. The rain pounded on the roof. It was coming down harder than ever.

"Yes, he was lucky. He could've been seriously injured

if he'd struggled too much," Sidney's mother replied. Her ginger hair was plastered to her forehead, and she shivered visibly.

They had found Magic tangled in an old, barbed-wire fence in the woods behind their house. The horse had a long scratch on his front leg. He'd been shaken up and nervous, but otherwise unhurt. Mrs. Fitzpatrick had inspected the wound and let out a sigh of relief. "It's not deep," she'd said, rain dripping from her nose. "I'll get him home and take care of it."

She had led the jumpy horse away and Sidney and her mom had returned home to rest and recuperate from the adventure.

"Let's change clothes and get a hot drink and breakfast," her mother said. She sent Sidney off to her room to shower and change into dry clothes while she did the same. When Sidney returned to the kitchen, her mother was wrapped in a fluffy pink bathrobe and wore matching slippers. Sidney wore plaid lounging pants and an overlarge T-shirt.

Her mother made a pot of coffee for herself and cup of hot tea for Sidney. She added a spoonful of honey to the tea, just the way Sidney liked it.

Sidney stirred and sipped the warm liquid gratefully while her mother cooked bacon, eggs, and a large pot of oatmeal.

After she finished her tea, Sidney got an apple from the fridge and sliced it up. She added the slices of apple and a generous pinch of cinnamon to each of the bowls of oatmeal her mother set on the table.

"Delicious," her mother said, taking a small bite. The steaming oatmeal tasted wholesome and filling. By the time the meal was eaten, Sidney felt renewed.

Her mother suggested they retire to the living room to

watch a movie and talk. Sidney picked out the only horse movie she owned: The Black Stallion. She popped it into the DVD player and cuddled up on the couch underneath a blanket.

The rain continued to come down outside, but Sidney felt warm and comfortable under the blanket. Her mother came to sit next to her and they watched the movie in silence for the first half hour.

"I have a question for you, Sid," her mother said finally, interrupting a brilliant riding scene in the movie.

Sidney tore her eyes reluctantly from the TV screen. "Yes?"

Her mother looked at her seriously. "You seem to really enjoy riding. Would you be interested in taking more lessons?"

"More than one lesson a week?" Sidney asked, her heart soaring. This sounded like it was going to be good.

Her mother nodded and reached down to brush Sidney's hair back from her face. "Yes. Mrs. Fitzpatrick was talking to me while we were out looking for Magic. She needs some help around the stables. She was impressed with your quick thinking last night and was wondering if you might like to do a little bit of work there. In exchange, she would give you an extra riding lesson every week."

Sidney sat up and put her arms around her mother. "Would I! Of course, I would love to work at Blue Moon Stables. I would get to be around the horses even more."

Her mother nodded and laughed. "Yes, you would. It'll be a great learning experience if you're really interested in sticking with riding."

"I've never been more interested in anything in my life," Sidney exclaimed.

"That's what I was hoping to hear. I'll call Mrs.

Fitzpatrick and let her know. She said she'd like you to start sometime next week."

Sidney settled back down into the couch cushions while her mother phoned Mrs. Fitzpatrick. She smiled sleepily as she watched the Black Stallion gallop across the TV screen. Everything seemed to be going her way.

CHAPTER 6

The Accident

Sidney wasn't able to make it to the stables again until the next Monday. She'd meant to go over and check on Jasper and Magic the day after their escape but her father had managed to make it down for a visit, and Sidney couldn't bear to tear herself away from him.

In fact, Sidney got so wrapped up in family activities and catching up with her father, she put her new job out of her mind entirely until that Monday morning when she woke up with nervous flutter in her stomach. After a hurried breakfast with her parents, she headed off to work feeling very grown up, and more than a little scared.

Sidney spent the next hour or so learning the ropes. Mrs. Fitzpatrick showed her how to muck out stalls, clean tack, and turn the horses out to pasture.

The horses had already been fed when Sidney got there, but after she'd finished polishing the last saddle, Mrs. Fitzpatrick decided to show her how to do that, too.

A wooden ladder was built right onto the wall in the tack room and led to a hole in the ceiling.

"That's the barn loft," Mrs. Fitzpatrick said. "It's where the hay is stored. Want to go up?"

Sidney nodded enthusiastically. Was this really supposed to be work? She loved being in the barn all day.

She clambered up the ladder with Mrs. Fitzpatrick

right behind her. The top of the barn was open, not split into stalls like the floor below, and it was entirely filled with square bales of sweet-smelling hay.

Mrs. Fitzpatrick walked forward cautiously. "You have to be very careful when you are up here," she said. "You see these?" She motioned to what looked like trap doors in the floor. There were three of them spaced evenly on either side of the loft.

Sidney nodded.

"Open one," Mrs. Fitzpatrick said, watching Sidney with her hands on her hips.

She hadn't bothered with makeup, but Sidney thought she looked pretty. She had her dark brown hair pulled back into a ponytail, and the exertion of working in the barn, along with the cool morning air, had made her cheeks rosy. She almost looked too young to be Bryan's mother.

Sidney leaned down and pulled on a brass ring attached to the trap door, lifting it up. She peered into the hole.

"It's Misty's stall!" she cried, surprised. "What's it for?"

"What's right below the hole?" Mrs. Fitzpatrick replied with a grin.

"Oh!" Sidney said, looking down. "The hay manger. So you don't have to take the hay downstairs? You just open these doors and feed the horses from here?"

Mrs. Fitzpatrick nodded. "That's right."

The hay mangers were already full so Sidney closed the little door.

"I love your stables, Mrs. Fitzpatrick. I'm so glad you're letting me work here."

Mrs. Fitzpatrick led the way back to the ladder and swung herself down gracefully onto its rungs. "I'm glad to have you. I thought Bryan might like to help. I was going to give him extra on his allowance for doing some chores in the barn, but he doesn't seem to want any part of it."

"He seems to like the riding lessons," Sidney said. "I thought he liked horses."

She was still angry with Bryan but hadn't let on to Mrs. Fitzpatrick. He hadn't been out to the barn all morning, so she hadn't been forced to talk to him.

"Well, I think he only participates in the lessons because he gets to ride with other kids his age," she replied. "He misses his friends back home. I'm glad to see he and Jimmy are getting along well. And he and Jane have been spending quite a lot of time together."

Sidney sighed. "You mean when he came over to my house?"

Mrs. Fitzpatrick smiled and stood waiting at the bottom of the ladder for Sidney. "And yesterday when he went over to see her. And the day before that. He absolutely loves those dogs of hers. It's all he's been talking about. I might look into getting him a puppy for his birthday."

Sidney frowned and climbed down slowly, being very careful where she placed her feet. She had always been just a teensy bit afraid of heights. "I didn't know Bryan and Jane had been playing together. I guess I've been busy. My dad's working out of state, but he's in town visiting for a while, so I've been spending most of my time with him."

Knowing that Jane had been playing with Bryan without her hurt her for some reason. She felt betrayed.

"Well," Mrs. Fitzpatrick said, "you've done some really good work this morning, but summer should be for fun, too. Go home and enjoy the rest of the day. I'll see you tomorrow. You can feed the horses in the morning if you'd like."

Sidney smiled and thanked her. "I would love to feed the horses. I'll see you tomorrow, Mrs. Fitzpatrick."

She started down the barn aisle, but her instructor stopped her. "Oh, Sidney. We need to be very careful about latching the gates and stall doors. And keep your eyes out for anything... out of place."

Sidney nodded, confused. "Of course."

Mrs. Fitzpatrick hesitated for a moment, a troubled look in her eyes. "I'm just telling you because of the other night. The horses getting out of the pasture."

"I thought you said that was a problem with the fence?"

Mrs. Fitzpatrick nodded. "It was. A part of the fence was down. At first, I thought a deer or something had knocked it down."

"But it wasn't a deer?"

"I'm not sure what happened. The fence looked so cleanly cut... It almost looked intentional."

"Like the tack room?"

Mrs. Fitzpatrick flinched and shook her head. "I hope not, Sidney, but we need to be careful. Just keep your eyes out for anything out of the ordinary."

Sidney assured her she would and tried to smile at her riding instructor bravely, but a shiver ran up her spine, and Bryan's words echoed through her mind once again. *This place is cursed...*

* * *

By Wednesday, Sidney had gotten into a routine. She woke up early, just after sunrise, and made her way to the barn. She fed the horses through the hay slots in the loft, watered them with the hose in the barn aisle, then picked the manure and soiled wood shavings out of the stalls, adding new shavings when needed.

The fact that wood shavings covered the stall floors instead of straw confused and disappointed Sidney at first. In the books she'd read and the movies she'd seen, the horses always stood in deep beds of straw. But the fresh-smelling wood shavings grew on her quickly. When she spread them out on the floor, they made a springy, sweetly scented bed for the horses.

After working in the stalls, she would help Mrs. Fitzpatrick prep horses for lessons, scrub buckets, or clean the barn aisle.

Mrs. Fitzpatrick didn't require this of her or even ask for her help. In fact, it was the other way around. In her eagerness, Sidney would ask to help Mrs. Fitzpatrick beyond what was required of her, and Mrs. Fitzpatrick sometimes refused on the grounds that Sidney had put in so much effort that day already.

That's exactly what happened that Wednesday. After finishing all her morning chores with the horses, Sidney asked to stay and help out around the barn before the group lesson began at eleven.

"Sidney," Mrs. Fitzpatrick said, shaking her finger at her student, "you need to go home and eat breakfast. It's not good to ride on an empty stomach. Besides, isn't your father leaving soon? You need to spend some time with him."

So, much to her dismay, Sidney was forced to return home for breakfast. Her mother and father were sitting at the table with empty plates in front of them when she got home. Her father folded his newspaper up and smiled at her.

"How was work, ladybug?" he asked.

She went over to give him a hug. "Great!"

He laughed and kissed her on the cheek. He smelled

like cologne, and his hair was still wet from the shower. He had the same brown eyes as Sidney, but, unlike her, his hair color matched his eyes. Sidney thought he was probably the handsomest father she had ever seen, but her friends had been known to say differently. They all favored their own fathers.

"I wish I could be so enthusiastic about my job," he said. He wrinkled his nose. "You sure smell like you've been working. Did you muck out stalls, too?"

"Yes. I do every morning."

He raised his eyebrows. "I'm impressed. Trying to prove that you're ready for your own horse?"

Sidney's mother gave him a look and shook her head at Sidney, whose eyes had gone wide. "Don't even start thinking about it yet, Sid," she said. "We're not going to consider getting a horse until you've been riding for a full year and some of the glamour has worn off. We have to see that you're going to stick with it."

"Yes, because what could be more glamorous than mucking out stalls?" Sidney laughed.

"You have to admit, Sid," her father grinned, "you've been a little flighty with your hobbies in the past."

She made a face at him and went to the sink to wash her hands.

Her mother gestured toward the counter. "Breakfast is waiting. And we're having a special dinner for your father tonight, so no going to play with Jane after the lesson. You need to come back here so we can all spend the day together. Your father has to go back to Philadelphia tomorrow."

Sidney frowned. She hated it when her father left for work. "Okay."

* * *

She got back to the barn about fifteen minutes before her lesson was scheduled to begin. With Mrs. Fitzpatrick's permission, she went ahead and groomed Jasper. Then she brought all her tack from the tack room and set it outside the stall door.

Bryan came out soon after she had accomplished this task and began his preparations with Magic. He didn't speak to Sidney when he walked by, and she didn't offer a greeting either. His dark brows were knitted furiously over his brown eyes, and his face was set in a grim frown, but he dealt with Magic gently and knowledgeably, which Sidney admired. They passed each other several times in the barn aisle, but neither gave any sign of having seen the other.

If Mrs. Fitzpatrick noticed their coldness to one another, she didn't address it. She was busy preparing the arena for the lesson.

Jimmy showed up at almost exactly eleven, and Sidney was happy to see him. Having another student in the barn relieved some of the tension in the air.

She started putting Jasper's tack on, wondering where Jane could be and why she hadn't shown up yet. It was the first lesson they hadn't walked to together, and Jane was late.

Just as she finished tightening the girth on Jasper's saddle, Jane appeared breathlessly in the stall door. "Morning, Sidney."

"Where have you been?" Sidney asked, taking in Jane's excited appearance. "Mrs. Fitzpatrick's tacking up Misty for you. I wasn't sure you were coming."

"We had to take Snapper to the vet this morning. We just now got back. The waiting room was crazy."

"Is she okay?" Sidney asked, concerned.

Jane nodded but didn't have time to talk. Mrs.

Fitzpatrick called for her to come and take over Misty's preparations and told the rest of the students to head into the arena. It was time for the lesson to begin.

* * *

At one end of the arena, Mrs. Fitzpatrick had set out three white poles on the ground. On the other end, she had put out two barrels about twenty feet apart.

"Now that we have a little time in the saddle," Mrs. Fitzpatrick said to the group, "I think we can move on to some riding exercises. There are students in this group at different riding levels, and you're riding horses at different levels."

She paused and leveled her gaze at Bryan, who actually had Magic standing still for once. "I'm looking at you, Bryan," she said. "You know Magic can be spooky around the poles, so be careful."

Bryan nodded and patted Magic on the neck.

"Okay. Let's go. Jane and Sidney, practice doing figure eights around the barrels. Bryan and Jimmy, I want you walking and trotting over the poles. Take turns."

Jane and Sidney did as they were told, steering their horses toward the blue barrels on the right side of the arena. Jasper seemed to know this exercise by heart and required little direction from Sidney. Jane sat on Misty and watched while Sidney walked figure eights around the barrels.

"If he's doing well at a walk, try trotting," Mrs. Fitzpatrick called to her. Sidney nudged Jasper with her heels, and he picked up the pace to a slow trot. She steered him carefully around the barrels.

"It's hard to stay at a trot!" Sidney gasped, squeezing her legs tightly to his sides..

Jasper felt lazy and bored beneath her. His hooves

even dragged in the dirt.

"Keep him moving," Mrs. Fitzpatrick said, coming over to their side of the arena.

Sidney pressed him harder, and he moved into a quick trot, shooting forward faster than Sidney expected. He clipped one of the barrels with his shoulder when they passed, and it teetered, almost falling over. Sidney groaned and tried to pull him out wider around the next one, barely succeeding. She knew her seat looked terrible. She bounced all over the saddle.

"It's alright," Mrs. Fitzpatrick said. "That was good. You're learning. Let Jane take a turn."

Jane walked Misty around the barrels several times and then urged her into trot. Misty navigated the barrels gracefully, sticking close to them but never brushing against them or threatening to knock them over. Jane rose up and down easily in the saddle in perfect rhythm with Misty's trot.

"Excellent, Jane!" Mrs. Fitzpatrick clapped her hands. Jane, startled by the compliment, lost her timing and bumped hard against the saddle, wincing. Mrs. Fitzpatrick counted, "One, two. One, two. One, two," loudly and Jane quickly picked up the rhythm again.

"It's like dancing," Jane said to Sidney as she passed. Sidney smiled back. It did look a bit like the horse and rider were dancing together.

After about fifteen minutes, Mrs. Fitzpatrick called for the two groups to switch. Jane and Sidney walked their horses across the arena toward the poles. As they passed the boys, Bryan pulled alongside Jane. He reined Magic down, and Jane did the same with Misty. While Jimmy and Sidney practiced on the poles and barrels, their two friends sat talking in the middle of the arena.

Sidney was curious, but she tried to ignore Jane and

Bryan and focus on Jasper instead. He was doing well, picking his way through the poles on the ground carefully, when a loud thud startled both horse and rider. Jasper jumped to the side, almost unseating Sidney. She tightened up on the reins and sat deep in the saddle, just as Mrs. Fitzpatrick had told her to do in such a situation. The horse settled down almost immediately and stood still, his hooves between the poles.

Sidney turned to see what had happened and saw Jane sprawled on the ground. Bryan was trying desperately to calm Magic, who was dancing around nervously, and Mrs. Fitzpatrick was running over to the scene of the accident, leading Misty. The gray horse's nostrils flared and her sleepy eyes appeared alert and even frantic. The saddle wasn't on her back anymore. It lay in the dust about a foot from Jane.

Sidney started to urge Jasper toward the scene, but Mrs. Fitzpatrick quickly put up a hand. "Everyone keep your distance. Just keep your own horse calm and stay away."

Their instructor kneeled next to Jane, who lay unmoving on the ground. Sidney's heart fluttered nervously, and she wiped her hands on her jeans, realizing how sweaty they were when the reins almost slipped through her fingers.

Luckily for her, she did not have to calm Jasper. He stood and watched the furor with interest but no fear. Magic, on the other hand, continued to give Bryan a run for his money. Bryan had the horse's head pulled around almost to his side, and the pair turned continually in circles like a top.

Jane finally stirred and groaned, holding her arm. Sidney sighed with relief. She looked across at the other students. Jimmy looked suitably concerned and watched the unfolding scene with interest. Bryan's face was white and strained and, though he still battled with Magic, he had all his attention on Jane.

Sidney could see Jane's mouth moving and could see Mrs. Fitzpatrick talking back to her, but she couldn't hear what was said. Finally, Mrs. Fitzpatrick stood up and helped Jane to her feet. Her left arm was cradled to her side, and she was covered with dirt from the arena. Mrs. Fitzpatrick shot a worried glance at her other students and led Jane through the gate and out into the barn, guiding her with a gentle hand on her back. She returned a moment later.

"I would like for you to all dismount your horses and put them away. The lesson is going to have to end early today."

"Is Jane okay?" Sidney asked, her voice cracking. Mrs. Fitzpatrick looked far too worried for Sidney's liking.

Mrs. Fitzpatrick nodded. "She'll be fine. She's on the phone with her mother now. Mrs. Abbot will pick her up and take her to the doctor."

"She's hurt then?" Tears pricked at her eyes and she tried to hold them back. Jane had never been injured badly enough to have to go to the doctor. She always played it safe. She'd never suffered a broken bone or even a sprained ankle.

"She's hurt her arm," Mrs. Fitzpatrick said. "Please dismount and put your horses away."

She watched while the students followed her instructions solemnly. Even Bryan refrained from rolling his eyes or laughing. In fact, he looked he might be sick to his stomach, and he stared at Sidney nervously.

Bryan and Jimmy dismounted slowly, but Sidney slid off immediately. She hurried Jasper to his stall, exchanged his bridle for a halter, and tied him to the brass ring in the corner. When she turned around to hang his bridle outside the stall, Bryan stood looking at her over the half door.

"What is it?" she snapped at him.

"I'm sorry," he said. "Won't you forgive me? I didn't mean to hurt you or Jane."

Sidney shoved the bridle into his hands. "Fine. You're forgiven."

"Really?" Bryan said hopefully. He hung the bridle on the saddle rack outside the stall door.

Sidney nodded, trying to follow her mother's directions and be nice. "Yes. Really. I'm sorry I ignored you."

Bryan shrugged. "I shouldn't have reacted that way. I know that barn is your and Jane's spot. You probably didn't want some stranger there in the first place."

Sidney didn't respond. She couldn't deny it. She paused and looked at Bryan with tears in her eyes. "Will you help me finish so I can go and see Jane? I want to be with her."

Bryan nodded. He let himself into the stall and helped her remove Jasper's saddle. Then he assisted her in rubbing the horse down, and he picked out Jasper's hooves while Sidney returned her tack and grooming supplies to the tack room.

When she got back, Jasper's stall door was shut, and he was munching contentedly on the hay in his manger. Bryan was back in Magic's stall finishing his grooming. Sidney hesitated, trying to decide whether or not to talk to Bryan. While she stood in the aisle, Jimmy backed out of Charlie's stall, loaded down with his heavy Western saddle.

He groaned and set the saddle on the saddle rack. He saw her watching him and smiled. "I'm sure Jane's okay,

Sidney. I'll see you both next week."

Sidney attempted to return the smile, but it didn't work and came off as more of a grimace. "Thanks, Jimmy."

Taking a deep breath, she walked over and peered into Magic's stall. The horse looked exhausted after his antics in the arena. "Thank you," she said quietly to Bryan.

"You're welcome." Bryan glanced up and smiled at her, but he still looked upset.

Sidney walked away reluctantly. She felt like she should say more to Bryan, but she didn't know what to say.

She hoped to see Jane outside, but she wasn't there. Mrs. Fitzpatrick stood in the driveway alone. Her clothes were covered in dirt from kneeling in the arena, and her face had smudges on it where she had rubbed it distractedly with her dirty hands. She looked at Sidney sadly.

"Jane just left with her mother," she said. "You should go home, too."

Sidney nodded, the tears finally cascading down her cheeks, and began the walk home, this time without her best friend.

CHAPTER 7

An Unexpected Finding

As soon as Sidney reached home, she told her mother about Jane's accident. Mrs. Sinclair immediately called Mrs. Fitzpatrick to see how badly Jane was actually hurt. She looked relieved after talking to the instructor and came to sit by Sidney at the kitchen table.

"It's only her arm," she said to Sidney, setting the cordless phone down. She rubbed Sidney's back comfortingly. "It might be broken, but she'll be just fine."

When her reassurances didn't calm Sidney, she tried to get her to eat some lunch, offering her anything she wanted in the kitchen, but Sidney couldn't stomach a single bite of food.

She sat miserably at the table with her head in her hands until the sound of a car turning into the driveway next door caught her attention. Sidney leapt up, almost knocking her chair over in her haste, and grabbed the doorknob to race outside, but her mother held up a hand to stop her.

"Let's not bother them yet, Sid," she said. "Give them a few minutes to settle in. I'm sure Mrs. Abbot is not in the greatest mood."

"But Jane…"

"Sid, don't argue. Jane's only injured her arm. She's not deathly ill." She raised her eyebrows and gave Sidney a look that meant she was serious.

Sidney's boots scraped loudly against the clean kitchen floor as she trudged back to her seat and plopped down, resigned.

Almost fifteen minutes had passed before her mother came over and put a hand on her shoulder. "Okay, let's go see Jane. We'll take her some cookies. She'll like that, won't she?"

Sidney nodded and wiped a tear from her cheek. She waited impatiently by the front door while her mother wrapped up a plate of double chocolate chip cookies.

They walked over to the Abbots' house together and knocked on the door. Mrs. Abbot opened it

"Hi, Laura," Mrs. Sinclair said, holding out the plate of cookies. "We brought Jane a little something. Sidney has been so worried about her."

"Thank you," Mrs. Abbot said distractedly, taking the cookies. "We appreciate it. Why don't you come in?"

Sidney looked up at her mother, surprised. Maybe she should always bring her along to Jane's house. She had never been invited so readily into the Abbots' home. And her mother had even called Mrs. Abbot by her first name, Laura. *That was brave*, Sidney thought. She had never heard anyone call Mrs. Abbot by her first name except Mr. Abbot. She knew Jane had gotten into a lot of trouble once for doing that very thing.

"We would love to," Sidney's mother replied. They followed Mrs. Abbot down the long hallway and into the spotless kitchen. Jane sat at the kitchen table sipping a steaming cup of hot tea. She had tear stains on her cheeks. Sidney gasped when she saw her friend's arm. It was covered in a white cast that went all the way from her hand up to her elbow.

"It's broken," Jane exclaimed as soon as Sidney walked

in. She sniffled back tears and wiped her swollen eyes with her good hand.

Sidney felt a pang of sympathy for Jane and ran over to give her a tight squeeze.

Mrs. Abbot sighed, "Don't be so dramatic, Jane. It's just a broken bone."

Sidney and Jane separated, but Sidney took the seat next to Jane and held her hand.

"Does it hurt horribly?" Sidney asked, eyeing the uncomfortable looking cast.

Jane shook her head negatively, her mussed hair swinging around her face and sticking to her wet cheeks. "No, it hasn't hurt since they put the cast on. Besides, they gave me some pain medicine at the hospital."

"That's good."

"Did you take care of Misty for me?" Jane took another sip of her tea. Sidney knew Mrs. Abbot gave Jane hot tea when she wanted to calm her down. Mrs. Sinclair did the same thing with Sidney, only she added honey and some sort of sweet treat as a side.

"Mrs. Fitzpatrick took care of her," Sidney replied. "Misty's fine, but Mrs. Fitzpatrick was pretty upset."

"Of course she was upset," Mrs. Abbot said. She poured coffee grounds into the filter inside the coffee maker then glanced over her shoulder. "My daughter was injured while in her charge."

After adding water, she banged the top of the coffee maker shut and came back to the table carrying two empty mugs from the cabinet. The coffee maker began to gurgle as it brewed.

"Well, they are riding horses, Laura. They're animals," Sidney's mother said. "They can be unpredictable. That's why we had to sign a release saying we understand that injuries can occur while riding."

Jane's mother shook her head. "I realize that, Cara. I'm just beginning to wonder if our girls should be riding those big horses. If accidents can happen so easily, it must not be safe."

Sidney gasped. Was she suggesting the girls stop riding?

"You know, Jane wanted to drop out after the first lesson," Mrs. Abbot said. "I should have let her. I told her to stick with it, but I think I was wrong. This is more my fault than anyone else's, I guess."

Sidney glanced at Jane and she looked guiltily away. She hadn't told Sidney she wanted to quit. *What else is she not telling me?* She tried to meet Jane's eye, but Jane stared stubbornly at the kitchen floor.

"I'm sure it's not anyone's fault," Sidney's mother replied. She took a seat at the table while Mrs. Abbot retrieved creamer from the refrigerator.

"I want to keep riding now," Jane said. "I don't want to quit."

"Well, you may have to quit, Jane," her mother replied. "Look at your arm. You can't ride like that."

Jane looked down at the hard cast on arm and shrugged. "How long will I have to wear this thing?"

"The doctor said six to eight weeks. That's a long ways away. Maybe you should quit riding for this year, and if you still want to try it next summer, we can discuss it."

"But Mom!" Jane yelled. She jerked her uninjured hand out of Sidney's grasp and slammed it on the table. "I want to ride this summer. Sidney gets to ride, and she gets to work there, too!"

Mrs. Abbot's mouth fell open. "Jane Abbot, you do not talk to me that way!"

She looked embarrassed and even turned a little red in the face. Sidney wasn't amused. She'd never heard Jane talk like that to her mother and it made her uncomfortable, too.

The coffee finished brewing, and Mrs. Abbot poured some for Sidney's mother and herself.

"Go play in your room, Jane," Mrs. Abbot said, eyeing Sidney distastefully. "Cara and I need to talk."

Jane got up and stomped to her room with Sidney on her heels. As soon as Sidney was inside, she slammed her bedroom door, threw herself onto her pink, ruffled bedspread and burst into tears. Sidney climbed up on the bed and put her arms around her.

"Don't be sad, Jane. You'll get better soon and your mother will let you start riding again."

"I don't know if she will or not, but that's not all I'm upset about," Jane said, gasping for breath. "It was so embarrassing. I ruined the lesson. Mrs. Fitzpatrick looked so scared and it was all my fault."

Sidney laughed. "That's a silly thing to be upset about. You were so brave. Everyone was impressed. You didn't even cry when you broke your arm. I would have." Jane whimpered and rubbed her eyes. She looked a little happier. "Really?"

"Really. Of course, we were all really worried about you. Jimmy and Bryan will want to see you and know you're okay. Even if you can't ride, you should come to the lesson next week and show them your cast."

Jane looked down at it. "It is pretty cool. The doctor said I could get all my friends to sign it."

"I want to sign it." Sidney jumped off the bed and searched through Jane's desk until she found a purple pen.

Jane watched while she drew a large heart and her name next to it.

"Draw a horse for me," Jane said, giggling.

Sidney complied and drew a horse somewhat clumsily. She had been practicing drawing them, but she hadn't gotten very good yet.

"Sorry. It's not great," Sidney said.

Jane smiled. "I think it's really good."

Sidney put the cap on the pen and returned it to its drawer. "Just before the lesson you said you were late because Snapper had to go to the vet, but you never told me what's wrong with her."

Jane gasped. "I can't believe I forgot." Seeing the worried look on Sidney's face, Jane quickly added, "She's okay. She's not hurt or anything."

"You told me that already, but if she's okay, why did you have to take her to the vet?" Sidney asked. She got up to look out Jane's bedroom window. The two German Shepherds were playing on the grass in the backyard.

"She's not sick," Jane said, following Sidney's gaze. "She's going to have puppies!"

"Puppies," Sidney replied, amazed. "Snapper's going to have puppies?"

Jane nodded and smiled. "And they should be here before the end of the summer. We'll get to play with them."

* * *

When Mrs. Sinclair finished drinking her coffee, Sidney was called back into the kitchen and told to say goodbye to Jane. "It's time to go home and let Jane get some rest," her mother said. Mrs. Abbot nodded in agreement.

Sidney said goodbye to her friend much more readily than she usually would have, eager to get out of the tense environment, and followed her mother out. As soon as they reached their own porch, Sidney sank down onto the nearest chair.

"Sweet tea?" Her mother said, glancing over at her.

Sidney nodded appreciatively, and her mother went into the house to retrieve it.

The screen door squeaked loudly when she opened it and slammed shut behind her.

Sidney laid her head against the back of the chair and closed her eyes. The days were growing warmer all the time, and she realized her shirt was sticking to her body with perspiration. She sniffed her shirt and made a face. It smelled like sweat and horses. She hadn't even showered after coming back from the barn.

Her mother returned a minute later with a glass of sweet tea for Sidney and ice water for herself. She sat back down in the chair next to Sidney and sighed.

"Poor Jane."

Sidney took a sip of the cool, sweet liquid. It felt refreshing and, after a sip or two, she regained a little bit of her energy. She pressed the cold glass against her hot skin and closed her eyes.

"I know. I'm glad I have you as a mom and not Mrs. Abbot," Sidney replied.

Her mother laughed, but she didn't look displeased. "That isn't what I was talking about, Sidney."

Sidney grinned, but it faltered when she thought about Jane's tearstained face. "Do you think Mrs. Abbot will really make her stop riding?"

Her mother shrugged and frowned. "I'm not sure. She seemed pretty serious about it. She doesn't like horses, you know. She only encouraged her to do it because she's friends with Mrs. Fitzpatrick."

The screen door banged open and Sidney's dad poked his head out. "I've got the steaks grilling out back and the baked potatoes on. How's Jane doing?"

Sidney looked up at her dad and frowned. "Dad! She's fine, but you weren't supposed to cook your special dinner! We were! That's why it's special."

Her dad smiled and perched next to her on the chair. He put his arm around her. "No. It's special because you're here."

* * *

The next day, Sidney's father dropped her off at Blue Moon Stables on his way to the airport. He kissed her quickly before she got out of the car. "I'll see you in a few weeks, ladybug."

She climbed out and blew him a kiss. "I'll call you tonight."

She skipped off toward the barn while he turned the car around to head back down the driveway.

For the first time, Mrs. Fitzpatrick didn't meet her at the barn door. In fact, she wasn't in the barn at all.

Sidney shrugged, figuring Mrs. Fitzpatrick had just slept late, and started her chores. She climbed up into the hayloft and fed all the horses from above. Then, she turned on the water hose and filled each horse's bucket to the brim. She cleaned out the stalls and made sure every horse had plenty of shavings.

Just as she was finishing up, Mrs. Fitzpatrick finally came in, but she barely glanced around the barn. "Are you done, Sidney?" she asked. Her voice was strained and she looked distracted.

"Yes, ma'am," Sidney replied. "I think so."

"Good," Mrs. Fitzpatrick responded quickly. "I need to talk to you and your mother. Would it be okay if I took you home instead of you walking? Do you think your mother will have time to speak with me for a moment?"

Sidney nodded, confused. Mrs. Fitzpatrick's hair was

in its usual ponytail, but it looked messy, like she had put it up in a rush, and dark circles hung heavy beneath her eyes.

"Sure. Mom said she was just going to work in the garden today." Sidney followed her riding instructor to the blue pickup truck and hopped up in the passenger seat.

Mrs. Fitzpatrick backed slowly down the driveway instead of turning around and pulled out onto the road, driving forward for the few yards it took to get to Sidney's driveway. Her mother looked up, surprised, when the truck turned in the drive and rushed over, obviously worried. It seemed Jane's accident had put her more on edge than she had let on.

Sidney jumped out as soon Mrs. Fitzpatrick had come to a stop.

"Is everything okay?" her mother asked, trying to keep her voice even.

"I'm fine," Sidney said. "Mrs. Fitzpatrick gave me a ride home because she wanted to talk to you."

"Actually, I want to talk to you both," Mrs. Fitzpatrick said, getting out of the truck.

"What about?" Mrs. Sinclair peeled her green gardening gloves off and stuffed them into the back pocket of her work jeans. Her knees were covered in soil from the flowerbed, and her face looked a bit grimy.

"Jane's accident," Mrs. Fitzpatrick replied. She sighed and shook her head. "I guess I shouldn't say accident after all. It appears that's not what it was exactly."

"Not an accident?" Sidney's mother knitted her brows. "What do you mean?"

Mrs. Fitzpatrick took a deep breath, and with a pained look in her eyes, continued on. "Jane did not fall off the horse by accident. She didn't just slip off because the horse spooked or bucked."

"What do you mean, Mrs. Fitzpatrick?" Sidney asked. She felt nervous butterflies fluttering in her stomach. This didn't sound good.

Mrs. Fitzpatrick frowned. "What I'm trying to say is…" she paused and took a deep breath, "someone sabotaged her."

Sidney's mother laughed and looked at Mrs. Fitzpatrick like she had lost her mind. "Don't you think that's a little dramatic? Why would someone want to do that to Jane?"

Mrs. Fitzpatrick shook her head. "I don't know why. All I know is it was done. Someone tampered with the girth and made it so it would break once Jane started riding. I don't know when it happened, but the girth did *not* break on its own. It was too cleanly cut for that."

Mrs. Sinclair put a hand on her hip. "That's crazy and very dangerous. Surely one of your students wouldn't do that? None of them even know Jane very well besides Sidney."

Mrs. Fitzpatrick agreed and looked forlornly at the ground. "I don't know. I've thought about it all night. I decided to go around and tell all the parents in person. I checked the girth just before she mounted, but it must have been cut on the opposite side. I never thought…."

"You can't blame yourself," Mrs. Sinclair said. She reached out and patted the riding instructor's arm.

"It's hard not to, but I want you to know that I will check each and every girth thoroughly from now on. I will check every bridle and saddle blanket. I will personally supervise as every horse is tacked up. Nothing like this will happen again."

"But Mrs. Fitzpatrick that'll take forever! We'll barely get to ride if you have to watch every single person tack up," Sidney exclaimed.

"I'll make sure you get to ride, Sidney," Mrs. Fitzpatrick said. "But I can't have another child get hurt on my farm. If it happens again, I will be forced to close my doors."

Sidney's face paled and she looked in fear at her mother.

"Shouldn't Jane have noticed her girth being so badly cut when she put the saddle on?"

Mrs. Fitzpatrick shrugged. "I don't know how she didn't. I brought the saddle out myself and was just about to put it on Misty when Jane came in. The girth was fine then. I'm sure of it. I don't know what could have happened to it between the stall and the arena. I'm going to talk to Jane and her mother next."

Sidney's mother looked sympathetically at Mrs. Fitzpatrick. "I hope it goes well."

"I do, too. I don't want to lose Jane as a student."

"I don't want you to either, Mrs. Fitzpatrick," Sidney said. Sidney grasped her mother's hand and looked up at her riding instructor, who smiled back grimly.

"Thanks, Sidney. I'll see you at your private lesson tomorrow, right?"

Sidney nodded and Mrs. Fitzpatrick put a hand on her shoulder and looked her in the eyes. "Do you know anything about this, Sidney? Anything at all? If Jane talked to anyone about it, it would be you."

Sidney frowned. "Of course not, Mrs. Fitzpatrick. Jane will be shocked. This is crazy."

Mrs. Fitzpatrick let out a long breath. "Yes, it is."

"I appreciate the fact that you came over to talk to me." Mrs. Sinclair smiled encouragingly. "We'll be sure to let you know if you we hear anything."

"I appreciate your understanding. I suppose I'd better

go and speak with Laura and Jane now." She said her goodbyes and walked over to the Abbots' house with determined steps. She knocked on the door, and Sidney and her mother watched as Mrs. Abbot answered and invited her in. She wasn't exactly friendly, but she didn't seem angry either. Not yet, anyway.

Sidney sighed. "I feel bad for Mrs. Fitzpatrick."

"I do, too, Sid," her mother replied. "I do, too. She's had a lot of bad luck lately."

"Maybe it's more than bad luck, Mom. Maybe it's the curse."

"Curse? Mrs. Fitzpatrick isn't cursed, Sid. A real person cut that girth and probably because they either wanted to hurt Jane or Mrs. Fitzpatrick."

"But who would want to do that?"

Her mother shook her head. "I don't know, but she needs to find out before something more serious happens."

CHAPTER 8

The Horse Detectives

After Mrs. Fitzpatrick left, Mrs. Sinclair went back to gardening and Sidney went inside and showered, washing the sweat and the smell of horses out of her hair.

She dried off afterwards, feeling refreshed, and pulled on blue jean shorts and a white T-shirt. Gathering up her dirty clothes, she made her way to the laundry room and tossed her smelly garments onto the wash pile.

Herbert sat next to his food bowl, which had been filled to the brim. His water bowl was full as well.

"Good afternoon, Herbert." She patted the cat on the head. He hissed and ran away. Sidney pursed her lips as she watched his tail flick around the corner and disappear. She was beginning to doubt she would ever find a way to get along with that cat. He just didn't like her. He tolerated Mrs. Sinclair petting him, and occasionally even Mr. Sinclair, but never Sidney.

She pulled on her boots and ran outside. The screen door banged shut loudly behind her. Mrs. Sinclair stood up and wiped the sweat from her face. "Just about done, Sid," she said with a smile.

Sidney surveyed her mother's work. The plants had all been trimmed back and appeared neat and orderly. Most of them were just beginning to bloom and little bursts of color could be seen up and down the flowerbed. Weeds were heaped on the sidewalk in a refuse pile, ready to be thrown out.

"It looks great, Mom. Thanks for feeding Herbert for me," Sidney said. "I forgot to fill his bowl this morning before I went to the stables."

Her mother grinned at her and Sidney giggled. She had a large smear of dirt streaked across her chin. "You've taken on a lot of responsibility this summer. How about if I take care of Herbert for a while?"

"Really?" Sidney asked, leaping down the front steps. She threw her arms around her mother and squeezed her. "You're the best."

Mrs. Sinclair laughed and stretched her arms over her head. "Time to go in and rest. It looks like rain."

Sidney looked up. The sky directly above them was still a clear blue, but not far away steel gray clouds had begun to form. They seemed to be heading in their direction.

"It looks like it'll be a nice summer thunderstorm," her mother said. "What are you doing for the rest of the afternoon, Sid?"

"I wanted to talk to Jane about what Mrs. Fitzpatrick said," said Sidney. "I'll come home right after. I'm pretty tired after working this morning. I'd like to rest, too."

Her mother nodded and went to fetch the wheelbarrow while Sidney wandered off toward the Abbots' house.

Sidney found Jane in the backyard playing fetch with the dogs. She looked much more cheerful than she had the previous day.

"Hey, Sid," she called when she saw her peering over the fence. "Come in."

Sidney unlatched the gate and went to sit beside her. She was relaxing in a pool chair and tossing the red rubber ball across the yard with her good hand whenever Snapper or Sam brought it back to her.

"Did Mrs. Fitzpatrick come talk to you?" Sidney asked, although she already knew the answer.

"Yeah," Jane replied. She didn't look upset.

"Did she tell you about the girth?"

Jane nodded. "Yes. Can you believe it?"

"Not really. Why would anyone want to hurt you, Jane?"

Jane shrugged and accepted the red ball from Sam, who had pushed his nose into her lap and slapped a big paw onto her knee. She tossed the ball across the yard, and the two dogs took off after it.

"I have no idea."

"You didn't notice the girth was cut when you saddled Misty?"

Jane thought for a minute, biting her lip. "No, I don't remember seeing anything out of place. But I didn't actually saddle her myself."

Sidney tried to catch Jane's eye, but Jane avoided her gaze, focusing instead on her game with the dogs. It had gotten to the point where it was almost impossible to sit in the backyard without playing fetch with them. They constantly pestered everyone with their ball, begging for it to be thrown.

Sidney pushed Snapper away as the dog tried to drop the ball on her lap instead of Jane's. *Jane didn't saddle Misty?* Sidney felt a pang of fear shoot through her. *What if it's Mrs. Fitzpatrick's fault after all?*

"Who saddled her, Jane?" she said out loud, trying to keep her voice calm.

"Mrs. Fitzpatrick had groomed her and everything and had her tied in the stall ready to tack. It still takes me a while to tack her up by myself. On his way into the arena,

Jimmy saw me struggling and offered to help."

"So Jimmy tacked her up? Mrs. Fitzpatrick didn't say anything about that," Sidney said. She felt somewhat relieved, but also confused. Jimmy would have known the girth wasn't safe if he had put the saddle on Misty. Was he covering for someone or did he cut the girth himself?

Sidney's mind whirled with questions. She knitted her brow. She couldn't believe Jimmy would be the one to cut the girth. Why would he want to? He barely knew Jane or Mrs. Fitzpatrick.

Jane interrupted her thoughts suddenly, "Actually, I don't remember who actually put the saddle on. Jimmy tied Charlie outside the stall and came in. Bryan was right behind him and did the same. You know how he follows Jimmy around." Jane rolled her eyes. "They tacked her up together. It only took a few minutes. I don't think Mrs. Fitzpatrick even noticed. She was getting the arena ready and setting out poles or something."

Sidney frowned. So it could have been either of them, or they could have done it together.

"You don't seem upset that someone did it on purpose."

Jane was actually smiling.

She shrugged. "It was probably just a joke." She saw the look on Sidney's face and sighed. "Yes, it was a terrible joke, but no one is out to get me."

"Jane!" Sidney said. "Accidents happen, but this was intentional. Besides, what will your mom think? Is she going to let you ride at a place where someone intentionally tampered with your riding equipment?"

"Well, she's upset that someone did it on purpose, but now she's more concerned with finding out who did it and punishing them than with keeping me from riding. Now that it isn't my fault or Misty's fault, she can't stop me from riding."

Sidney chewed on her lip absently while she thought about Jane's words. What had happened wasn't really Jane's fault, although she should have checked her own girth before getting on the horse. And it definitely wasn't Misty's fault. However, it didn't make Sidney feel any better to know that someone had tried to hurt Jane on purpose. In fact, she felt more scared and upset than when she thought it was just an accident.

A raindrop landed right on the tip of Sidney's nose. She shook it off and Jane laughed, looking up. "It's about to get nasty out here," she said. "We better go inside."

"I think I'm going to go home. I'm really tired after working at the barn this morning. Are you still coming to the lesson next week?"

Jane nodded. "I'm planning on it. I asked Mrs. Fitzpatrick if I could come and watch the lesson She said it would be fine."

"I think we should figure out who did this ourselves," Sidney said, getting up from her chair. "Your mother won't let you keep riding at the same place where someone tried to hurt you. Besides, the girth cutter could hurt somebody else. If we find the culprit, it'll be safe. You can start riding again as soon as your arm heals."

Jane agreed reluctantly. "I still don't think it's that big of a deal. And did you just say "culprit"?"

Sidney shook her head. She couldn't believe Jane could be so nonchalant about it. "I've been reading a lot of detective books lately."

"It shows."

Sidney stuck out her tongue and made a face at her friend. She might be going little overboard with the whole thing, but had to admit, she was excited at the idea of playing detective.

* * *

The next Wednesday, Sidney hurried through her morning chores at Blue Moon Stables then waited impatiently outside the barn for Jane. She thought her friend might need support in facing the other students, one of whom may have sabotaged her saddle.

However, Jane's steps looked spry as she approached and she smiled at Sidney when she got close enough. "Ready to ride?"

Sidney nodded and frowned. "I wish you were riding, too."

"It won't be too long." Jane linked her good arm with Sidney's and they walked into the barn together.

Mrs. Fitzpatrick stood in the center of the barn aisle with a clipboard in her hand and a grim look on her face.

"Before we even touch the horses, I want to talk to everyone in the arena," she called out. She looked serious. Her mouth was set in a grim line and her face was pale.

The girls followed her slowly into the sandy arena. Bryan and Jimmy already stood in the center, looking apprehensive.

"All right," the riding instructor said. "We have a serious problem here. You all already know what it is and what happened last week."

The students all nodded in unison. Sidney snuck a look around. Bryan looked upset and pale like his mother. His thick brows were lowered, and his face was full of tension and anger lines. Jimmy looked confused and a little worried. He kicked at the ground with his booted toe nervously and little puffs of dust flew up, dirtying his boots and jeans.

"I will not have someone playing such dangerous pranks," Mrs. Fitzpatrick continued. "Jane was injured and, frankly, it could have been much worse. If it was one of you who did this, I expect you to come forward and tell me. I will not be angry. I'll talk to your parents, and we'll figure something out. You may not have known how dangerous it could have been, but now you do."

She looked around expectantly at her students. They stared back at her silently.

"Well, I just want to let you know that I have lost students due to this incident. I've already had two students drop out of other classes. After the stunt that was pulled last week, their parents have decided to remove them from riding lessons at Blue Moon Stables."

Jimmy kicked the ground particularly hard at this news and dirt flew forward, showering Mrs. Fitzpatrick's pants. She pursed her lips and stared at him. He blushed and stammered out an apology. "I was just surprised is all," he said. "I can't believe anyone's parents would make them leave here just because of one accident."

"Well, that's just it," Mrs. Fitzpatrick responded. "It wasn't an accident, was it? We have a student here who purposefully tried to hurt another student. I have to say, I can't blame their parents for being worried. However, I am determined not to let this happen again. I will be personally supervising as each of you tack up today. This checklist," she said as she held out the clipboard in her hand, "has each of your horses and their tack listed on it. I will watch you tack up, inspect each horse, and sign off on it. You will then sign your name at the bottom to assure your parents I followed through with it. You will be responsible for your horse and your tack after that, and you are not to leave them alone without telling me. We will not give anyone the opportunity to play the same trick again."

Jimmy looked upset, and Bryan sighed and rolled his eyes. Jane and Sidney looked at one another grimly. It sounded desperate.

Mrs. Fitzpatrick watched them all closely. "Do you understand?"

The students responded positively, and she led them back into the barn. Sidney thought the tacking up process would take longer than usual, but since Jane wasn't riding and Bryan and Jimmy were very quick about it, they actually managed to be out in the arena by their usual time.

The lesson was uneventful. Jane watched from the sidelines while Sidney practiced posting. She was getting better, but still had a lot of work to do.

"And up and down, and up and down, and up and down," Mrs. Fitzpatrick called from the center of the arena. Sidney tried to stay in rhythm with her voice. Her legs were not used to the exercise and they grew more wobbly and exhausted with every passing moment. She knew she'd get it down if she kept at it, though, and the posting trot felt much more comfortable than the sitting trot.

"Your private lessons are really helping." Mrs. Fitzpatrick smiled. She motioned for Sidney to halt and walked over to stroke Jasper's neck. "I'm impressed."

Sidney grinned so widely and enthusiastically it almost hurt.

"I'm going to work with the boys for a while. I want you to keep practicing your posting. I'll be keeping an eye on you."

Jimmy and Bryan, who were more advanced and riding Western instead of English, practiced going between poles and around barrels while Sidney continued to trot around the perimeter of the arena.

Sidney stopped to watch them occasionally, admiring how they handled their horses, and sometimes Mrs.

Fitzpatrick would have one of them demonstrate something for Sidney.

All in all, she enjoyed being in lessons with Bryan and Jimmy, even thought they didn't always get along. She knew she could learn a lot from them, and they weren't stingy with their knowledge or advice.

After the lesson, Mrs. Fitzpatrick supervised while the students untacked their horses and returned their saddles and bridles to the tack room. Since Sidney was the slowest to finish untacking her horse, she was the last person in the tack room. She shut the door behind her and noticed a large padlock hanging from the handle.

Mrs. Fitzpatrick came up beside her and snapped the padlock shut. "No one will be getting in there without a key," she said with forced cheerfulness.

She patted Sidney on the shoulder. "You did very well today. I hope you're still enjoying riding here?"

Sidney nodded and beamed at her instructor. "Very much, Mrs. Fitzpatrick."

"Good," her instructor replied. "I know these rules are a pain, but as much as I hate it, it appears they are necessary."

Sidney nodded. "Don't worry, Mrs. Fitzpatrick. I know the rules won't be necessary for long. We'll find out who did that to Jane."

Mrs. Fitzpatrick looked at her doubtfully. "I hope so, Sidney. But it's not for you to worry about. These are my stables, so I need to take care of it."

She pointed toward the bin that held the horse treats. "Why don't you give Jasper a treat? He was a pretty good boy today."

* * *

The air had grown humid, and Sidney wiped sweat

from her brow. "I can't believe it's this hot already," Sidney said. "The summer's going to be over before you know it."

Jane nodded. "I wouldn't mind. Still five more weeks until I get this thing off." She held up her cast. She'd stuck around while Sidney finished up her barn chores after the lesson, and Jimmy and Bryan had both signed the cast and drawn silly cartoons on it while they waited. Jimmy's drawings looked a little goofy, but Bryan's were actually pretty good.

"Maybe the girth cutter is someone from another class," Jane said suddenly. She paused to pick up a rock from the driveway and tossed it halfheartedly toward a nearby tree.

Sidney made a face. "How? Mrs. Fitzpatrick said the girth was fine when she brought the saddle out to the stall."

Jane frowned. "Who do you think did it, then?"

"I'm betting it was Jimmy," Sidney said with confidence. "I've been thinking about it, and he seems like the most likely candidate. I like him, but he's a jokester. He probably loves pranks and just didn't realize it would be so dangerous."

They walked up Jane's driveway and around to the backyard. Sidney let them in the gate. It was too hard for Jane with her cast.

Snapper and Sam jumped up on them, panting and whining, until Jane pushed them away and told them to sit. They did so obediently, and Jane searched around on the ground until she found their ball. She tossed it across the yard. The two dogs took off after it.

Jane shook her head and frowned. "I don't think it was Jimmy. He seemed awfully upset when he saw the messed up tack room."

Sidney shrugged. "So did Bryan."

Sidney tapped a finger against her chin. "I know what we can do. We can make a list of suspects like in the books. Then, we can mark off the ones we don't think did it. That might give us a clearer idea. Sometimes it helps to write things down."

Jane agreed and ran into the house to get some paper and a pen. Sidney heard screeching from Mrs. Abbot about "wiping your shoes on the mat before coming into the kitchen!" and giggled.

When Jane returned, they sat in the pool chairs closest to the pool. The water rippled and glinted invitingly in the sun. The pool was open now, but with all the excitement going on at the stables and now with Jane's cast, the girls hadn't even had a chance to swim in it yet.

Jane handed Sidney the pen and paper. "Your handwriting is better than mine."

"Okay. I'm putting Jimmy at the top."

She penciled in Jimmy's name at the top with Bryan's name scribbled just below it. Sidney then added Mrs. Fitzpatrick reluctantly.

"That's everyone who was there," Jane said, satisfied.

"Not quite." Sidney added her own name at the bottom.

Jane raised her eyebrows. "Who do we want to mark off first?"

"Mrs. Fitzpatrick. She would have nothing to gain from it. She lost you as a student and other people, too."

Jane sighed. "That's true. My mother has been telling everyone she meets. You'd think she would be a better friend to Mrs. Fitzpatrick. I don't think she is being mean, though. I think she just likes the drama of it."

"Probably," Sidney said. She drew a large X through Mrs. Fitzpatrick's name.

"I think you should mark yourself off, too, Sid. I don't know why you even put yourself on there. You know you didn't do it."

Sidney giggled. "They always put *everyone* on the lists in the movies." She drew an X through her own name.

Jane looked troubled. Sidney glanced up from the list, her smile faltering. "What's wrong, Jane?"

"You didn't put me on there," Jane replied quietly.

Sidney wrote Jane's name in cursive below her own. She marked a large X through it quickly.

"So, it's like we thought before," Sidney said. "Either Bryan or Jimmy cut your girth. They're the only possibilities."

"This list was silly," Jane sighed. "We wouldn't make good detectives, Sid."

Sidney crumpled the paper up and dropped it on the ground. "It was pretty useless, wasn't it?"

"Totally pointless."

Sidney snorted. "I've just always wanted to make a list of suspects, though."

Jane smiled. "It would be better if we had more suspects."

Sidney agreed and sat thinking silently for a minute. "I think we need to talk to Jimmy and Bryan. Maybe one of them saw the other do it, and they're just too scared to tell."

CHAPTER 9

Wet Paint

The next morning, the air was already heavy with humidity when Sidney went out to the feed the horses. She sighed and looked up at the sky. She knew the heat would only get worse, and the humidity more oppressive, as the day went on.

She'd probably be exhausted after completing her barn chores, but she made a mental note to stop by the house and talk to Bryan afterwards. She was determined to find out exactly what he knew about the incidents at Blue Moon Stables. She wouldn't be able to question Jimmy until their next riding lesson, but Bryan would be at home. The hard part would be getting him to talk.

Sidney made her way up the driveway slowly, the sweat already beginning to form on her brow. The barn looked quiet and peaceful. The door stood open and a horse looked curiously out of each stall, ready for breakfast.

A chorus of whinnies greeted Sidney. Jasper nodded his head up and down enthusiastically, and Jasmine, Jasper's sister, reached as far as she could over her stall door to try and nibble Sidney's shirt sleeve. Jasmine craved attention. She wasn't being ridden by any of the riding students at the moment, only Mrs. Fitzpatrick, and the young horse seemed bored in her stall. Mrs. Fitzpatrick had bought her from Jasper's former owner only a few weeks before Blue Moon Stables opened. She was quite a bit younger than Jasper and still in training.

"She's still green," Mrs. Fitzpatrick said when Sidney asked her why no one ever rode the beautiful black mare. "I want to get her a little more seasoned before I put students on her."

"Green?" Sidney had asked incredulously. "And you're going to season her? Like food?"

Mrs. Fitzpatrick had laughed at the look on Sidney's face and explained that the term "green" meant a newly broken horse, one without much experience under the saddle. "And when a horse trainer talks about a 'seasoned' horse," Mrs. Fitzpatrick had told her. "They mean one with a lot of experience. Most of my riders are beginners and aren't ready to ride a horse like Jasmine."

Sidney stopped to stroke Jasmine's nose. "Poor sweet thing," she whispered to the little mare. It was obvious she and Jasper were related. She looked just like a smaller version of him. "You just want somebody to take you out and ride you, too, don't you?"

Jasmine whinnied softly. Sidney kissed the horse on her velvety nose and headed toward the tack room. She patted Jasper on the nose as she passed.

The air up in the loft felt thick and suffocating. She took a deep breath and rushed through the chore of feeding the horses. When she climbed down, she shook the hay from her clothes and pulled out the watering hose. She filled Jasmine's water bucket first, watching the cold water swirl around and slowly rise up the sides of the bucket. It looked cold and inviting, like the clean, clear water in the Abbots' pool.

When the bucket had filled to the brim, she pulled the hose out and glanced around guiltily before turning it on herself. She let the cold water run down her arms and wash away the tickly feeling the hay always left behind, then she stuck her face into the stream and rinsed the sweat away.

It felt heavenly. She sighed with relief and reluctantly pointed the spray toward the next empty bucket.

She was humming quietly to herself while waiting for the bucket to fill when a sound in the driveway outside the barn caught her attention. It sounded like the crunching of gravel beneath a foot. She turned quickly, but no one was there.

She shivered, a creepy feeling coming over her. The feeling that someone had been watching her.

The horses didn't seem to notice. They were still distracted by the hay they'd just been given.

She finished filling the buckets as quickly as she could and put away the hose, then she went to investigate.

The sun had risen higher in the sky. It felt warm against her wet skin. She looked around curiously. Nothing seemed out of place.

Then she noticed it. A paintbrush. Wet, red paint covered the bristles and splotches of red paint splattered the blades of grass and the dirt around it. It looked like someone had thrown it down. She walked over and picked the brush up. If the paint was still wet, someone must be nearby.

She glanced around then took a few hesitant steps toward the side of the barn, still holding the brush.

She nearly tripped over the paint can. It sat open, almost hidden in the tall grass, with the top discarded on the ground beside it. "Hello?" she called, thinking Mrs. Fitzpatrick must be up and about after all. No one answered.

She edged around the barn slowly, feeling something just wasn't right. When she saw it, she gasped.

A message had been written on the side of the barn in large red letters. The paint had dripped in places, and the letters were all uneven, but the message was clear, "GET OUT!"

Her jaw dropped. She stood stock still, stunned, in front of the hateful words.

"Sidney?" Mrs. Fitzpatrick's voice came from around the side of the barn.

Sidney almost dropped the brush and turned just in time to see the bewildered look on her instructor's face as she came around the corner. She read the message silently then turned to look at Sidney.

"Why, Sidney? I don't understand," Mrs. Fitzpatrick said slowly, her face losing all its color.

Sidney looked down at the brush in her hand, suddenly realizing how it must look.

"No, Mrs. Fitzpatrick. It wasn't me."

Her riding instructor looked at her sadly. "Lying isn't going to do you any good at this point, Sidney."

Before Sidney could respond, Mrs. Fitzpatrick turned and walked away. Sidney stood by the barn uncertainly, unsure of what to do. Tears pricked at her eyes, and she did all she could to hold them back.

Finally, she put the brush down slowly and left everything as it was. She felt like she should clean it up, but she thought that would just make her look guiltier.

She figured Mrs. Fitzpatrick had gone to call her mother, and she was right. She waited outside the barn until her mother arrived, looking angrier than she had ever seen her. She slammed the car door when she got out and stomped over to where Sidney stood.

"Sidney," she said. Her voice was quiet, but Sidney could hear the seriousness in her tone. "Did you do this?"

Sidney shook her head slowly but definitely. "I didn't,

Mom. Mrs. Fitzpatrick made a mistake. Let me show you."

She took her mother by the hand and led her around to the side of the barn. The painted letters had dried in the sun and were no longer shiny and wet, but the bright red words still stood out starkly against the rough brown wood of the barn.

"I picked up the brush because I found it over there. Mrs. Fitzpatrick walked up just after I found it. I was holding the brush. I know it looks like I did it, but I didn't. You have to believe me."

Sidney's mother bent down and looked her in eyes for a long minute. Sidney met her gaze steadily.

"I believe you, Sidney," her mother said finally. She got to her feet and led Sidney to Mrs. Fitzpatrick's front door and rang the bell.

Mrs. Fitzpatrick answered the door with a stony look on her face. "I'd appreciate it if Sidney did not return for lessons any more. I will no longer be needing her help in the barn, either," Mrs. Fitzpatrick said.

"I can understand why you think my daughter did this, but I think you're wrong. Sidney did not paint that on the side of the barn. She told me so, and I believe her."

Mrs. Fitzpatrick raised her eyebrows. "Well, you can believe her if you like, but I don't. She was standing right there with the paintbrush in her hand. I don't know why she would want to do such a thing, but I know she did it. There's no one else here."

She looked down at Sidney and shook her head. "You were such a promising rider, too."

Sidney had to fight the tears back. *I'll never see Jasper again,* she thought, *except at a distance. I'll just have to watch him grazing in his pasture and dream about riding him.*

Sidney saw Bryan peeking around his mother. He

looked afraid. His eyes were as wide as saucers. Sidney noticed that although it was still very early, he was up and fully dressed.

"My daughter didn't do this," Sidney's mother said again, her voice rising. "I'll have you know that she is not a liar."

Mrs. Fitzpatrick just shook her head. "Please go. I have quite a bit of cleaning up to do."

Sidney grasped her mother's hand, and they started to turn and walk down the front steps.

"You know, Sidney," Mrs. Fitzpatrick said suddenly. "This means you must have cut Jane's girth, too. Your best friend. Why would you do such a thing?"

"I would never do that to Jane, Mrs. Fitzpatrick. You're wrong."

"Well, then who did?" Mrs. Fitzpatrick said, stepping out onto the porch. "Who cut the girth if you didn't, Sidney?"

Sidney burst into tears and covered her face. Her mother put an arm around her shoulder, glaring daggers at Mrs. Fitzpatrick.

Bryan stepped out onto the porch behind his mother. He tugged at her shirt, and she brushed him away absently. "Who did it? Just tell me, Sidney. Admit it."

Bryan tugged a little harder, and she glanced down at him. "Stop it, Bryan," she snapped.

Bryan stomped his foot suddenly. "Listen to me! It was me, Mom."

All eyes turned to Bryan. "What was you, Bryan?" Mrs. Fitzpatrick asked.

"I did it. I cut Jane's girth."

He hung his head and wouldn't meet any of their eyes. He shuffled his booted feet nervously.

"You did it, Bryan?" Mrs. Fitzpatrick said quietly. She

didn't sound like she believed him.

He nodded and there was a long, uncomfortable moment of silence.

"Did you paint that message on the barn as well?" Sidney's mother asked grasping Sidney's hand so tightly it was almost painful.

Bryan nodded reluctantly again and looked up at Sidney. "Yes. I did it. I can't let Sidney take the blame."

Sidney's jaw dropped for the second time that morning.

"The tack room, too? You're the one who trashed it?" Sidney asked.

Bryan nodded and blushed.

"And the fence? You let the horses out?"

"I didn't know Magic was in there. I thought Jasper would just walk out and eat a little bit. Then we'd go get him. I didn't mean for it to be such a big deal."

"I've heard that a lot lately," Sidney muttered.

"Why, Bryan? Why would you?" Mrs. Fitzpatrick had turned all her attention to her son and didn't even seem to notice Sidney or her mother's presence any more.

"Because I hate it here, Mom," Bryan said loudly. "Haven't you noticed?"

Bryan looked up at her, tears filling his eyes. "I want to go home. You took me away from all of my friends. I just want to move back. I'll never like it here."

Mrs. Fitzpatrick put a hand over her mouth, and tears filled her eyes as well. She looked devastated, and despite all the mean things she had said to Sidney, Sidney felt terrible for her.

Sidney looked up at her mother. Mrs. Sinclair had won the argument, but she didn't look happy. In fact, she was looking at Bryan and his mother with a strange, sad expression.

"I think we should leave, Sid," she said. Her voice sounded strained.

Mrs. Fitzpatrick gestured quickly for her to stop. "Sidney didn't have any part in this?" she asked Bryan.

Bryan looked up at Sidney again. Sidney could see the pain and sadness in his eyes. "No, she didn't. She didn't know anything about it."

"I see," Mrs. Fitzpatrick responded. She turned reluctantly to Sidney and her mother, looking embarrassed. "I'm so sorry, Sidney."

Sidney couldn't think of anything to say. She shrugged her shoulders and turned to her mom. "Can we go home?"

* * *

Sidney stayed in her room for the rest of the day. Not because she was punished or because she had to, just because she didn't feel like leaving it. She curled up on the bed with one of her favorite books and lost herself in the story, forgetting all about her terrible morning.

Her mother brought snacks up to her occasionally. One time she told her Jane wanted to see her, but Sidney told her mother she didn't feel like talking.

She stayed successfully hidden in her room for the entire day, reading and watching movies, with only the occasional interruption from her mother. Mrs. Sinclair had been very sympathetic, but by the end of the day she was tiring of Sidney's seclusion.

Sidney stayed in her room until night fell then went to sleep. The next day, Sidney planned on doing the same thing, but a loud knock on her bedroom door at about ten in the morning interrupted her plans.

"Jane's here," her mother said through the door. "She says she's not leaving until she talks to you."

Sidney sighed and looked around her room. It was trashed. Her lock-in the day before had resulted in quite a mess. Empty plates from lunch and dinner sat on her dresser, and a half-eaten bag of chips was still open on her bedside table. Her mother had left the mess, hoping Sidney would tire of it and bring her dirty dishes downstairs.

"Fine," Sidney yelled a little louder than necessary. "Send her up. I don't want to come down."

She heard her mother's footsteps retreating slowly. Sidney knew Mrs. Sinclair wouldn't put up with much more.

Jane knocked softly on the door a few minutes later, and Sidney yelled for her to come in. Jane entered the room unhurriedly, reluctantly almost, and glanced around at the mess. "Hi," she said quietly. She came over to sit beside Sidney on her bed. The sheets were twisted, and the comforter rumpled where Sidney had tossed and turned.

"I heard what happened," Jane said. "I'm sorry, Sid."

Sidney pulled her fingers through her tangled hair, realizing she must look terrible. "It's not your fault. It's Bryan's fault. He's the liar. He's the one who framed me."

Jane sighed and went into Sidney's bathroom. She came back out with Sidney's hairbrush and tossed it on the bed. Sidney picked it up and went to work on her hair.

"He didn't frame you, Sid," Jane replied. Sidney had pulled an entire row out of the bookcase while trying to find something to read the day before, and Jane straightened the shelf up while she talked. "He didn't mean for you to pick up that paintbrush."

"Jane," Sidney said, ripping the brush through her hair painfully in her anger. "I was the only person there.

Whenever it was discovered, it would have looked like I did it anyway."

Jane paused and tilted her head thoughtfully. She wore a long necklace and matching earrings. Her parents had allowed her to get her ears pierced on her birthday. Sidney had begged her own mother at the time, but Mrs. Sinclair had been unrelenting. Sidney wouldn't be allowed to pierce her ears until she turned twelve.

Sidney felt a pang of jealousy and anger course through her. Why was Jane sticking up for him?

"I don't think Bryan thought of that," Jane replied. She went to Sidney's closet and pulled out a clean pair of jeans and a T-shirt. She tossed them on the bed in front of Sidney.

"I think we need to talk. Get dressed." She smiled and held her nose. "And for goodness sake, take a shower." Taking the hairbrush from Sidney, she ran it through the tangled strands until they were smooth then held out a closed fist in front of Sidney's face. "There was an animal cracker in your hair."

She giggled and Sidney smiled. "No, there wasn't," Sidney stood up. "I don't even have animal crackers up here."

"No," Jane admitted. "But it made you smile. And there could have been. There could have been a whole bird's nest in there and you wouldn't have noticed! Look at yourself."

Sidney glanced in the mirror for the first time since the previous morning. Her hair now looked presentable, but she had large dark circles under eyes, and her clothes were rumpled and dirty. She hadn't even bothered to change since working in the barn. She had just come home and crawled straight into bed. Smudges of dirt, and what was probably manure, stained her jeans. Her shirt had a blotch of red paint on the front. She made a face.

"Right," she said. "Shower."

Jane laughed. "I'll be waiting downstairs."

CHAPTER 10

The Truth is Revealed

Sidney felt much better after she cleaned herself up. She made her way downstairs slowly, stopping to sniff the air halfway down. Bacon.

When she entered the kitchen, she saw her mother sitting with Jane at the table. Both had tall stacks of blueberry pancakes in front of them, and a heap of perfectly browned bacon was set temptingly on a platter in the middle of the table.

"Mom," Sidney said, looking at her mother's smiling face. "What is all this?"

"I thought your favorite breakfast foods might cheer you up a bit," she replied, taking a large bite of pancake. "I even made blueberry syrup."

Sidney filled a plate with pancakes, smothered them with blueberry syrup, and poured a cold glass of milk.

"Thanks, Mom," she said as she sat down in an empty chair between Jane and her mother. She leaned over to give her mom a peck on the cheek. "You're the best."

Her mother smiled even wider and sipped her coffee.

"I'm glad you think so," her mother replied. She glanced at Jane uncertainly. "We need to talk, Sid."

Sidney took a small bite of crisp bacon and waited for her mother to continue. Jane set her fork down and stopped eating.

"Bryan and Mrs. Fitzpatrick came by yesterday afternoon," her mother said. "They wanted to talk to you."

"Well, you know I don't want to talk to either of them," Sidney replied. "I didn't yesterday, and I don't want to today. Or ever."

Her mother nodded. "I know. That's why I didn't even tell you yesterday when they came by, but I did talk to them myself."

"And?" Sidney said, stabbing a blueberry with her fork with unnecessary force.

"And it seems there is more to the story."

"What does that mean?" Sidney asked.

Jane looked down at the table. "It means that I knew what was going on, Sid," Jane said quickly.

Sidney paused in the middle of chewing to stare at Jane. "You knew what Bryan was doing?"

Jane nodded slowly, her blonde hair swinging back and forth. "Yes, I knew. When he started coming over to my house, he told me."

"So you knew he cut your girth?" Sidney asked, setting her fork down as well.

Jane glanced at Sidney's mother, who nodded encouragingly.

"Yes, Sid," Jane said. "I knew."

Sidney stood up from the table quickly, and her fork clattered to the floor. "And you just pretended like you didn't. You lied to me, too?"

Sidney's voice rose, and she clenched her fists angrily at her sides.

"Sidney," her mother said firmly. "Sit down. I will not have you yelling."

Sidney sat down slowly, but her hands were shaking.

Jane frowned. "Sidney, I didn't just know that he did

it. I planned it with him."

Sidney gasped and felt like she might choke on her surprise. She couldn't believe her ears.

She looked to her mother. Her mother nodded. Jane had already told her everything.

"Why?" Sidney choked out. "Why would you want to do that?"

Jane glanced down at the decorated cast on her arm. "I wasn't supposed to get hurt. We were going to stage it, like in a movie. We thought if I knew I was going to fall, it would be safe. It was stupid."

Sidney's mother nodded in agreement. "It was very foolish. It could've been much worse."

"I know, Mrs. Sinclair," Jane replied. Her large, blue eyes filled with tears, and she reached for Sidney's hand. "I'm sorry, Sid."

"Why did you want to fall at all?" Sidney asked, pulling her hand out of Jane's reach. She didn't feel like making up and pretending everything was okay when her best friend had lied to her and tricked her.

"Bryan hates it here," Jane replied. "He misses his friends. He wanted to go back home. He thought if he staged accidents and messed up his mom's business, they would go back. I felt bad for him, so I told him I would help him. I was going to tell you after we were done."

"But Mrs. Fitzpatrick was so good to us, why would you want to ruin her business? You know being riding instructor is her dream. She told us so."

A few tears spilled down Jane's cheeks. "I know. I know how terrible it was now, but it didn't seem like it when it was happening. It was going to be funny tricks. We thought she'd just move back. Why couldn't she have started her business up there?"

Sidney's mouth gaped open. She couldn't believe how

silly her friend had been.

"What about Jimmy?" Sidney asked. "Did he know?"

Jane shrugged. "I think he might have guessed, but Bryan never told him what he was doing."

Sidney sighed. At least she wasn't the only one who had been out of the loop.

"So, what happens now?" Sidney asked. She felt tired and betrayed and just wanted to retreat to her room again.

Her mother smiled. "Now we thank goodness that no one was hurt too badly." She looked pointedly at Jane. "And start forgiving."

"Forgiving?" Sidney said incredulously.

Her mother nodded. "Forgiving, Sidney. Bryan and Jane made a mistake. Several mistakes, actually. But they are sorry now."

Sidney looked at Jane. She did look sorry, and she had suffered quite a bit of pain with her broken arm.

"I realize what we did was wrong and incredibly stupid," Jane said, hanging her head. "Can you ever forgive me, Sid?"

Sidney frowned and crossed her arms. "Maybe we can work something out."

* * *

Several weeks later, only days before Jane was scheduled to head back to boarding school, the pair sat by the Abbots' pool, their legs dangling in the cool water. Sidney wiped sweat from her brow and looked up at the cloudless sky.

"How was Jasper this morning?" Jane asked. She rubbed her arm gingerly. The cast had been removed the week before, and it looked oddly pale compared to the rest of her body. She was trying to get the arm to tan before she returned to school.

"Wonderful. As usual," Sidney replied. "I got to canter him, and it felt like I was flying, Jane. I can't wait until you can start riding again."

"Well, they do have a riding program at Graceland Academy. I'm planning on trying it out. If I get involved there and you keep taking lessons here, we can stay at the same level."

"That would be great," Sidney said. It had taken a few weeks and several heartfelt conversations, but Sidney had managed to forgive Jane and Bryan for their deception. She had even started working with Mrs. Fitzpatrick again and continued taking private and group lessons.

Bryan poked his head over the gate and yelled a greeting. Jane and Sidney turned around quickly. "Come in," Jane called.

He sauntered in, latching the gate behind him. He wore swimming trunks and carried a blue and white striped beach towel over his shoulder.

Bryan had been spending more and more time at Jane's house since "the second painting incident" as it came to be called. As a result, he seemed much less angry and lot more friendly. It turned out Bryan got the idea to paint something on the barn when Jane told him about the time she and Sidney painted the Abbots' house hot pink. For some reason, Mrs. Abbot seemed to think that made everything Sidney's fault.

"He never would've gotten the idea for his little tricks if it weren't for Sidney and Jane misbehaving and bragging about it," Mrs. Abbot said to Sidney's mother when they found out. Mrs. Sinclair didn't agree or disagree. She just smiled politely and steered the conversation to a nicer topic.

Jane's punishment for acting so irresponsibly had been yard work, which she hated. Sidney glanced around the yard. *She did do a good job, though*, she thought. The flowerbeds looked as pristine as flowerbeds can, and every inch of the pool area had been scrubbed meticulously.

"Perfect day for swimming," Bryan said, lowering himself onto the hot concrete beside Sidney. She glanced over at him and smiled. *If I've learned anything this summer*, she thought, *it's that friendship can be shared between more than just two people.*

One reason she had been afraid to befriend Bryan was because she thought he might like Jane better. She was scared of losing her best friend. It was silly now that she really thought about it.

Bryan had changed quite a bit over the last few weeks. He worked in the barn with Sidney now as part of his punishment. Both he and Jane had suffered through a very stern talking to from Mrs. Fitzpatrick, and Bryan's allowance had been cut for the rest of the year. His chores had also been increased. Helping Sidney in the barn was now one of his daily chores. He didn't seem to mind, though. He seemed to enjoy the company of the horses, even when he wasn't riding them.

Working together had given Sidney and Bryan time to talk and get to know each other better. She looked forward to having a good friend around during the school year. Jane was wonderful, but she missed her an awful lot when she left for boarding school.

Jane dropped into the water, splashing Sidney. She swam a few laps while Bryan and Sidney watched then came back to float in front of them, her hair plastered to her face.

"If it's so perfect, why don't you come in?" Jane teased.

Bryan stood up and backed up a few feet.

"No!" Sidney yelled, but he didn't listen.

"CANNONBALL!" he yelled and ran toward the pool. The splash when he landed in the water hit Sidney right in the face.

Bryan surfaced neatly, and he and Jane giggled while Sidney spluttered.

"So that's how it's going to be, is it?" Sidney said. She dropped into the pool.

"Yep," Bryan replied, swimming backwards to get away from her.

"Well, then," Sidney said, splashing her way toward him. "This is war!"

A splashing war ensued. There were no losers. Everyone got sufficiently soaked.

* * *

Half an hour later, the threesome climbed out of the pool, exhausted, and laid out on their towels, letting the sun's hot rays dry them off.

Just as Sidney began to doze off in the heat, a whining from the shed interrupted their sunbathing.

Jane sat up groggily and pushed her tangled hair out of her face. "It's the puppies."

Bryan sat up, too. "Can they come out and play?"

Jane nodded and clambered to her feet. She opened the shed door and Snapper and Sam ran out followed by six little puppies. They tumbled and fell over each other in their haste to get out into the sun and fresh air.

Sidney grabbed the littlest one as he passed and snuggled him close to her chest. "Hello, runt."

Bryan picked up the largest puppy, who had been lumbering along slowly at the back at the pack. He had a friendly face and a constantly wagging tail. He licked Bryan enthusiastically, and his tail thwacked against

Bryan's stomach.

"Have you decided what you're going to name him?" Jane asked. She was playing with the other puppies. Their little bodies were tangled together as they wrestled on the grass near the shed. Snapper and Sam had gone straight into the pool and swam in happy circles, looking content. They had more to do now than play fetch.

"No," Bryan asked. He had a happy grin on his face as he hugged his new puppy, rubbing the dog's thick fur. "I'd like to get to know him a little better before I name him. I can't wait to take him home."

Sidney smiled as she watched the pair. The puppy's tongue hung out the side of its mouth, and it seemed to be smiling right back at Bryan. They were perfect for each other. Bryan had found another great friend.

The sad, lonely boy who had moved in across the street had changed, and Sidney was beginning to think he even had best friend potential. She hadn't lost Jane at all. She had gained Bryan.

* * *

The day before Jane left to return to boarding school, the threesome met up again. This time they met at the old barn for a picnic.

After they finished eating, they spread out on the soft grass, stuffed full of ham sandwiches, chips, and homemade chocolate chip cookies. The end of summer had come, and it would be months before they would all three see each other again.

It was sad, but exciting at the same time. A new school year lay before them. The events of the summer would slowly fade in their memory, but Sidney hoped the friendship they had managed to form wouldn't.

Bryan would be attending Walker Middle with Sidney,

and she would continue to work and ride at Blue Moon Stables. Jane was excited about starting the riding program at Graceland Academy and promised to stay in touch. She would be back for the holidays, and they had already promised to have a group trail ride when summer rolled around again. They would all be ready for one by then.

And Dad is coming home soon, Sidney thought, smiling to herself. He'd gotten a new contract in a town only an hour away. It wasn't permanent, but he would be home for at least six months.

Yep, she thought, *there is a lot to look forward to.*

She propped her head up on her hands and looked at her two friends.

"You know," she said, sighing, "it's been a strange summer. A lot of fun but crazy, too. I think I'm going to be kind of glad to go back to school."

Jane laughed. "I never thought I'd hear you say that, Sid."

THE END

If you enjoyed The Mystery at Blue Moon Stables, check out this excerpt from the next book in the series:

The Riding Camp Riddle
(Sidney Sinclair Adventure #2)

Chapter 1

Summer Begins

"Are you ready to hit the trails?" Sidney whispered to her lesson horse, Jasper.

The handsome black gelding nickered and pressed his velvety muzzle into her hands, looking for treats.

"Not yet, silly," Sidney said, pushing his nose away gently. "You know you don't get treats until after the ride. I'll take that as a yes, though."

Sidney finished tightening the girth on Jasper's saddle and led him out into the barn aisle.

"Ready to go, Sid?" Jane called from just outside the barn. She was already tacked up and in the saddle. Bryan and Jimmy, their fellow riding students, stood near her holding their mounts by the reins.

Sidney and Jane had been friends and neighbors for a long time, but they'd only known the two boys since the previous summer. The four friends met when the girls began taking riding lessons from Bryan's mother, Mrs. Fitzpatrick, at Blue Moon Stables. Mrs. Fitzpatrick owned and ran the stables, which happened to be located just across the road from Sidney's and Jane's houses.

"So ready!" Sidney called to her best friend. "I've been waiting for this ride for weeks."

Jane laughed and rubbed her horse's neck. She rode a small gray mare named Misty. Misty always looked tired and had a bad habit of plodding along lazily if you didn't keep her interested and busy. At the moment, she looked almost comatose. Her eyes were shut tightly and her bottom lip drooped down, revealing grass-stained teeth.

"Misty's asleep again," Bryan complained, but he smiled at the horse affectionately. "That horse is so lazy it's ridiculous."

Jane tightened up on her reins, turning Misty in a circle to wake her up. "Where's Bear?" she asked, looking around. "I thought he was coming with us."

Bear, Bryan's German Shepherd puppy, loved to tag along on rides and would sometimes follow the riders around and around the arena during lessons.

"Probably with Mom," Bryan said. "He's been keeping pretty close to her lately. She's in the arena with *Kelsey.*" He rolled his eyes when he said her name.

He turned to wave as a car pulled into the gravel drive, and someone in the passenger seat waved back. Sidney didn't recognize the person.

The atmosphere at the stables had changed a lot in a year's time. Sidney had rarely seen strangers at the barn when she first began riding, but with an ever-growing number of new students and boarders, people came and went at all hours of the day now. The stables seemed to be busy all the time and Mrs. Fitzpatrick couldn't possibly teach all the students by herself. That's why Kelsey had been added to the staff as a junior riding instructor. Sidney hadn't talked to her much yet, but she seemed nice enough.

Sidney gathered up her reins in one hand and started to mount Jasper, but right as she put her foot in the stirrup, Mrs. Fitzpatrick walked up with Bear gamboling at her heels, his legs flailing in the uncoordinated run of a puppy. He wasn't even a year old yet but looked like a full-grown dog. When he saw Bryan, he galloped over and jumped up, placing his huge paws on Bryan's chest. Bryan grunted and pushed him off.

"No, Bear. Down! Get down!"

Bear slumped down to the ground and wagged his tail. Bryan shook his head and waved a finger at the dog. "You've got to stop doing that. You're just too big. You'll hurt somebody."

Bear rolled over on his back and began to wiggle in the dirt. He didn't look the least bit ashamed. Even Mrs. Fitzpatrick had to smile.

"That dog's a mess." Kelsey laughed as she approached the group leading a little black mare. The mare, Jasmine, was Jasper's sister. Mrs. Fitzpatrick had bought the two horses from the same farm. They shared many of the same habits and quirks, and both had a calm, reliable personality. Jasmine was a sweet horse, but she was much younger than her brother and still in training. Only experienced riders, like Kelsey, were allowed to ride her.

"Okay, kids," Mrs. Fitzpatrick said. "You look like you're all ready to go. Kelsey's going to be leading your trail ride."

Kelsey smiled and fidgeted with her riding helmet. She looked a little nervous, so Sidney smiled back encouragingly. She was petite, not much taller than

Sidney, and had wild blonde hair about the same shade as Jane's. Kelsey's hair was long and curly, though, while Jane's was straight and cut into a cute bob that framed her face.

Bryan started to protest, but Mrs. Fitzpatrick stopped him quickly with a raised hand. "No arguments. This is the first trail ride for some of you, and we have some fairly new riders in the group. You'll have an instructor along for the ride."

"I don't think she qualifies as a real instructor," Sidney heard Bryan whisper under his breath. "She's not even that much older than us."

Jimmy laughed softly and climbed up onto Charlie, his tall chestnut Quarter Horse. He settled into his Western saddle and patted Charlie on the neck. Bryan followed suit, but his horse, Magic, fidgeted and danced nervously beneath him.

Both the boys liked to ride Western, while Sidney and Jane preferred the English style of riding.

Kelsey swung gracefully into the saddle and grinned at the young riders from Jasmine's back. She and Jasmine looked good together. Sidney sighed and smiled at the pair. She couldn't help but feel envious of Kelsey. She looked so grown up and confident in the saddle. Like she belonged there.

"Come on, guys," Kelsey called to the little group cheerfully. "Let's get going!"

* * *

ABOUT THE AUTHOR

Kathryn B. Butler grew up in a small town in Tennessee. Kathryn began horseback riding at the age of seven and began writing at about the same time. Horses have influenced her writing from a young age and are often featured in her stories. Kathryn has a degree in journalism, but prefers writing fiction to non-fiction.

She loves to hear from young readers, so don't hesitate to contact her. You can email Kathryn at kathrynbbutler@gmail.com, or visit whataboutjelly.com for information on Kathryn and her other books.

37213115R10086

Made in the USA
Columbia, SC
29 November 2018